# MURDER AT THE RED DOG

## by

## John Herrman

DEADLY ALIBI PRESS LTD
Vancouver Washington USA

MURDER AT THE RED DOG  Copyright © 2001 John Herrmann

ISBN: 1-886199-14-0

Library of Congress Control Number: 2001090944

Deadly Alibi Press Ltd.
PO Box 5947
Vancouver, WA 98661-5947

Disclaimer:

## ACKNOWLEDGEMENTS

I want to thank dear friends whose support and suggestions helped me during the writing and rewriting of this story: Susan Newell, MarySue Carl, Paul Loumena, Andy Herrmann, Leslie Budewitz, Lisa and Bruce Mohr, Jessica Ambats, Margo Power and the late Donne Florence who could not hang around to see this into print.

FOR MACKIE

# Murder comes to Small Town America

*Kootenai Falls, Montana April 28, 1998... AP,NYC: Three murders in as many days have stunned this tiny and traditionally peaceful northwest Montana community of 2,500 located near the Idaho panhandle and sixty miles south of British Columbia.*

*Late on the evening of April 25th, Gilbert and Elizabeth Owen, a husband and wife, were shot to death in the small computer and electronics office at the rear of the Red Dog Saloon, a roadside tavern they owned and managed. Two days later, on April 27, apparently in a related incident, a woman visiting in a friend's home in the same community was shot once in the head with a large caliber weapon.*

*All three appear to be execution style murders, and the sheriff's department and Yaak County Attorney Vreeland Peachart believe the same individual or individuals are responsible. However, no information has been forthcoming concerning just who the suspects might be nor has a motive for the killings emerged.*

*According to Kootenai Falls journalist Brew Moore, a source close to the investigation, initial indications are that a Native American religious ritual may have been involved, as golden eagle feathers were found by Moore's dog at the scene of the Owen homicides. Other theories by townspeople include the possibility of a set-up by members of the Militia of Montana. "The people of Kootenai Falls are pressing hard for a quick resolution here," Moore says. "They are very uneasy with the slow process of investigations. I'd say that rather than truth, they want a fast arrest and conviction." Talk around the local, colorful Red Dog Saloon is of conspiracies and even of possible organized crime involvement. According to Moore, "In Kootenai Falls, all rumors begin at the Red Dog."*

*As for what lies ahead, Peachart, himself a native of the area, says he expects to make an arrest within the next twenty-four to forty-eight hours. That may quickly act as closure and bring this alpine community, at the heart of what remains of the American wilderness, back to its normal and idyllic state.*

*by Kate Wells*
*AP National Reporter*

# Chapter One

A layer of fog over the Elk River obscured the mountains beyond town as I crossed the bridge and descended into the dark streets of Kootenai Falls. It was a chilly Sunday morning and it would be another day indoors at the paper. From the west came the only hint of an outside world — the operatic wail of the Burlington-Northern, its left-right sweeping head lamp illuminating the fog as it moved along the river toward the town. It would grind slowly through, and out, and then curl east... a two-mile long ghostly arm moving beneath the white blankets of a bed.

Poor Jessie: tough life out here for your basic border collie. You work sheep for fifteen minutes here and there when your master has time, when you were bred to go one-hundred miles a day.

There are secrets between Jessie and me. I saved her and she saved me. But we don't talk about it, and all I ever see in her eyes is the kind of devotion only a few of us lucky ones could ever imagine.

I was surprised to find the lights on and the doors unlocked when I reached the office. I thought probably another avalanche had gotten some unlucky skiers, or maybe come down on the main highway over equally unlucky late-winter tourists motoring through God's country only to be snuffed out by that very god.

Tom Everett was standing at his desk, the phone receiver tucked against his cheek, held there by his raised shoulder. He was bending over an old railroad style desk writing, listening, writing more, listening again. He looked up as I scraped my chair, then he looked back down at his desk. Jess circled under my desk, found her spot and settled in for a nap. Good girl. Always such a good girl, I told her quietly. You speak too loudly, and right away she thinks there are sheep in the office to gather and put somewhere. So you speak softly and in sweet tones, and then she stays put, closes her eyes and sighs. Let me know when the sheep arrive, she'll tell you.

Roxy, that's Tom's wife and the head of ad sales, came over, her face pinched. A formerly handsome woman of a certain age, she took good care of herself, colored her darkish brown hair a dark blonde, wore serious makeup, dressed *a la mode*, which is very rare for women living in the Outback. "Murder," was what she said. Roxy is a talker, always ready for a good argument, so a single word depicting something as important as homicide was, to say the least, unexpected.

"Who?" I asked, battling Roxy back single word for single word. (Roxy and I often enjoyed a verbal *mono-a-mono*.) There hadn't been a murder in Yaak County for months. Not since a child was smothered, presumably by a parent who couldn't handle the infant's screaming. None of that has yet been heard in court, so I speak here exceedingly off the record.

"Two of them," she said. "The ones ran the Red Dog."

I sat back. Gil and Beth Owen. "What happened?" I had to push to get the words out.

She shrugged and looked up at the ceiling. "They're dead's all I know. Don't know how or why anyone would kill those two."

"What about Dennis? Is he all right?" Dennis O'Brien was employee at the back office business in the Red Dog building, a programmer and handy man, and an old friend of mine from the days when I taught journalism at the University of Montana in Missoula and yearned for a more natural existence. Dennis had been having problems with several local cowboy types who fancied themselves anti-everything and pro-white. Dennis' name is deceiving, as he was said to be three-quarters Hopi. Indians often have a hard time with some few folks in some places in the western states. A holdover, I think, from the Indian wars. There is a feeling among some men that they would have preferred to live in the eighteen hundreds... and the anti-Indian mood comes from identifying with the nineteenth-century West.

Dennis and I had become good friends while he was doing honors work at school. He is in fact the person who introduced me to the Kootenai Falls area and who told me once when I was anguishing about my life in New York that he would see to it that I found nirvana here in these mountains when I was finally in the mood.

"No word about him," she said.

I felt relieved at that. I said I'd just seen Beth Owen Friday night. "She came in and dropped off their ad for next week."

Roxy looked over at her husband and half mumbled, "You had a thing for Beth."

"We were friends," I said. "There's a difference between a *thing* and friendship."

"Right. And you had a *thing* for her." She smiled through her sad lines and patted my desk with a makeup-covered, liver-spotted hand. "You must feel terrible right now," she said with heavy irony, for in truth, Roxy Everett didn't ever give thought to how anyone felt; she was all business but with a heart of silver.

She turned and walked back toward her office off the main newsroom. Her manner was decidedly East Coast. She was in fact originally from Syracuse, New York. At times, locals were offended by her brusque, big-city manner. But in my experience, having lived in New York City for a long while, she was very laid back by comparison. Still, no culture is more laid back than that of western Montana, unless it is some tiny village in the snaky Outback of Australia in the heat of summer.

"Not a *thing*, Roxy!" As she went into her office, her back to me, her hands came up, fingers spread, waving a kind of "Okay, okay, I hear you, I hear you," and pulled the door shut behind her.

Tom was off the phone then and sitting at his desk. "Beth Owen was raped and she and Gil were shot in the head," he said. "At the Red Dog, late last night."

Things like that feel like hot gravel in your chest. You shake your head and you try to shake the idea away. And you do not look at your hands. If they are shaking, you don't know it because for the moment you can't feel them and you do not look down. You do not look at your hands or look down at anything. You do not look. You see nothing, and if you see nothing then you may be lucky and feel nothing... for a while. Not until the sting of the hot gravel in your chest takes over. It grows and it grows, and it hurts, but you know it will lessen and you will go back to being able to look at your hands and feel nothing.

When I think of the death of good friends I try to think instead of riding horses. The air, the sense of motion. The elegant smell of horses.


The Red Dog is the pub Gil and Beth managed and from where they ran a home programming and electronics business. Bloodstained now. Tragedy here includes death by falling rock, freeze, flood, bear attack and falls from mountains during hunting season, and now death by murder. But I suppose murder is one of the few human acts that exists as well in these remote mountains as on the East 60s of New York City.

We are all born with the capacity to kill. We lash out from the crib, grab whatever we can for ourselves. We try to suck the life out of our mothers and fill ourselves with it.

Some of us grow out of it, some do not.

"Gil and Beth.... Who'd do a thing like that to them? They

couldn't have had an enemy in the world," I said.

"Maybe it wasn't an enemy," Tom said. "Maybe a friend did it. Or maybe someone who didn't even know them." He looked up. "Why'd you say enemy?"

"I just always assume people murder people they don't like. If it was a hold-up, they got the wrong store," I said. We all knew that this side programming business probably has about two hundred dollars in the register on the day before Christmas, never mind a Saturday night in April. Any other time and you'd find a few quarters and a five dollar bill. In the saloon it was different. But that till was emptied every night at closing and taken over to the Owens.

This is the kind of mountain community where people are overjoyed at having a job, *any* job. The Owens sold a lot of TV cable and short lengths of wire, an occasional package of batteries and every other year perhaps even a TV set or one of those small satellite dishes to a transplanted Californian who can't live without HBO. In its way, Gil and Beth ran a kind of miniature Radio Shack store tucked into the rear of a busy bar.

Tom told me to get on the story, then he went back to the phone. I headed out with Jess in my Pathfinder back out onto Rock Creek Road. She hung her head out of the driver's side back window, narrowing her eyes against the wind.

I had driven into the office before seven on that blustery and silver Sunday morning in late April to start work on a feature about our mountain lion problem, Jessie bopping around in the back as usual. I drove down Rock Creek from my place with both back windows down for her and the air was icy on us both. Still, by noon it would warm to avalanche-generating levels. Ah, but working on a Sunday was more privilege than burden. It got me going, it got me out into the drama of weather. After too many years groveling for a living in the cement world of Manhattan, I had returned to paradise, and working for *The Mountain Inquirer* was a breeze, despite its small-town "if you scratch my back, I'll scratch yours" publishing policy.

The paper is based in Kootenai Falls, Montana, a small mountain village where you hear echoing between the mountains earthquake-like sounds of freight trains rolling through the valley instead of the war-like rumble of jet aircraft taking off. There is no major airport within a hundred miles of Kootenai Falls. In late April and May, the rumble of a mountain of ice, snow and rock can sound the same as a mile-long Northern Pacific carrying a hundred gray boxcars with Suzuki written across them.

My name is Brew Moore — not the jazz saxophonist, but I *was* named after him by my cabaret-singing mother. I am a winner of a Peabody Award, a National Book Award nominee, all of which has allowed me to turn my back on New York. The Big Apple is surely all that they say it is. But for me, turning toward these mountains was as easy a decision as deciding whether or not to shower on a steamy summer evening.

As most New Yorkers will tell you, they don't trust air they can't slice. But I now have blessedly invisible air, a few mountain lions, an occasional moose — and Jessie.

You can't miss my little log cabin. I have a few sheep for Jessie and me to work, sharpen our skills, breathe good, sweet (invisible) sheep-dip air. And should you come here looking for me, ask for Ellen or Teri at the Red Dog Saloon. They will point to my place, just down the road. My neighbors, Jake and Kathryn, recite their favorite line, that it is a pleasant walk to the Saloon, and a short crawl home. If you ask for me there, one of the Red Dog's regular bar gals will hand you a take-out go-cup of Moose Drool dark draught beer and point to the west.

My life went another way in the half year of being a small-town reporter, and meeting many of its citizens every day. The last place I lived was the trendy Upper West Side of Manhattan at 74th and Columbus Avenue, a few blocks from the Dakota where Yoko and John Lennon lived — and also where he died. It is the same neighborhood where Sigourney Weaver lives and where Chris Walken has a town apartment. I was one of a stable of feature writers at *The New York Post.* I was hired away from the obscurity of writing for *New York Magazine* by the *Post*'s bright young woman editor who said she was motivated by her infatuation with writers. "I just wanted to be around them," she confessed. Previously, she had been on the investigative reporting team of one of the best known newsmen of the last three decades. She brought me to *The New York Post* just days after she took over its editorship — one of only two or three women ever to edit a newspaper with a circulation over one-million. And because she is a very independent person, she didn't last long at the *Post*, and neither did I. After a few months I could not take the pace and the dreadful stories I was coming up with. A book I had been working on forever got itself a couple of months on the *Times'* best-seller list, which gave me all the dollars and options writers dream about most of their lives. So when I saw an opportunity to join a small village newspaper in the Montana Outback that had more concern for not offending local businesses than breaking news stories, I grabbed at it. What is life like at Kootenai Falls? In an issue of the paper here that I read before taking the job, three of the thirty or so items in the "Sheriff's Report" leaped out at me:

*2:15 p.m. — A caller reported that kids in a small blue Honda had thrown an egg at his house at 661 South Seeley;*

*3:50 p.m. — A caller reported that a man with a walker with his face painted white was talkin to windows on Main Street;*

*9:12 p.m. — A caller reported the theft of a bread maker, a black lunch bucket and an Nintendo game from a trailer on Colinga at the 800 block.*

Indeed — I would write happy stories of small-town successes by day, work our sheep by evening and on weekends, and tilt Moose Drool at the Red Dog and bitch to its managers about losing my quarters in their video poker machines. I would drink that exquisite draught dark beer brewed in Missoula and, because it's that kind of pub, eat major quantities of peanuts and throw the shells on the floor as everyone else did.

I left the office about 8:00 a.m. and drove out to the Red Dog slowly as there had been a build-up of ice from the snow a week before that had melted, frozen and melted and frozen again. As usual, Jessie was running around in the back between the left and right windows as we worked our way through the seriously pot-holed back streets toward the bridge. She'll race to the driver's side and stick her head out for a moment, then pull it in and move to the back where her bed is, and then dive for the right window. I always leave the Pathfinder's back windows down for her except when we're on two-lane highways and logging trucks are coming at us. They kick up stones and a lot of surface dirt, and I don't want Jess getting a rock in the eye or getting that pretty white face with the black Jesse James mask all muddy.

At the Red Dog, a detective from the sheriff's office, Toby Wales, was inside along with three highway patrolmen and some of my neighbors. And two sleepy dogs were being kept from the scene by clothesline tied to the front railing. At the right of the entrance to the back office there was a stack of TVs, a camcorder between them mounted on a tripod connected to a laptop computer, and dozens of smaller portable TVs, stereos, computer monitors, small radios and stacks of boxed audio and video tapes.

The bodies hadn't been moved. Toby nodded his pretend tough-assed hello without saying anything. If you come here from New York or California, you have a long haul before anyone accepts you as a member of the community. Oh, they smile and are polite and wish you a good day when they sell you something. But if you weren't born and raised here in Kootenai Falls, Coaler or Elk River, then you will always be the new guy in town. In all fairness, this is the case in many such villages across this country. But Toby was the exception; he had not found it difficult to fit in. He had a master's degree in law enforcement from the University of Michigan, and the people around here knew they were lucky to get him. It was a given that as soon as he was seasoned he'd run, and win, the job of Yaak County sheriff.

Beth Owen was lying on her stomach near the doorway to the back office, her legs spread, her jeans, underpants and white sneakers in a bundle near her head. She still had on short white cotton socks.

Gil was face down in a lake of blood near the entrance.

I stepped carefully around Beth's body and headed toward the back office. Official things in Kootenai Falls are casual to a fault, and Toby made no comment about my nosing around. In Manhattan I would by now have been kicked out of the store and told to stay behind the yellow crime-scene tape.

Two physicians from the local clinic showed up. In a village just getting the news that Doctor Welby is fiction, these two are called Doc Wes and Doc Pete, they are partners a the Kootenai Clinic, and both of them have been known to break their most important professional oath of "Thou shalt not make house calls." Neither Wes nor Pete was there in an official capacity, but the county coroner is not a physician, and since homicide is a rarity in Yaak County, Wales called for some expert help..

Doc Wes is Canadian — a youngish, bearded intellectual type family physician from the Yukon, with a stop in Berkeley for medical school who, if you met him at the Red Dog, you would think him in the logging business until he offers his views on why his kids aren't being taught to think in school. Then you witness a fine mind, obviously taught to think, exploding with documentation for his opinions. He has quick eyes and an appreciation of subtle humor. However, as with many Western men, he has become expert at never laughing at another man's joke. He will listen to your joke and then quietly offer a line like: "That's funny," delivered straight faced and with a barely discernible nod.

Doc Pete, a gastroenterologist who, because the clinic is

a three-person practice, covers for his pals and does ingrown toe-nails and acne and dishes out pain relievers to old white-bearded men who regularly fall on the ice and, when the pain is almost gone and they are bored with watching "Colombo" reruns, come to the clinic late Friday afternoons when two-thirds of the help is already into their weekend so someone, often as not Pete, has to hang on until closing time. The talk quickly turns from falls and pain to Carla in Elk City and the elk she got last year. Men line up on Wednesday and Thursday evenings at Sheila's Beauty Parlor & Antique Pickover, owned and operated by Carla Corlova, for five-dollar haircuts. But for that price one has to endure the story, over and over again, of how she got her last elk. She gets an elk every six or seven years, and once every other month for the next seven years each of her male clients will be entertained by how she stalked it, where her shot hit the poor beast, and who helped her drag six-hundred pounds to her truck. It's a blessing when she gets an elk, though, as you don't have to hear about who is screw-ing whom, and with what sort of equipment.

Wes and Pete went over the bodies and looked beneath eyelids, poked into ears, and I did not care to watch.

There are two desks in the back office and both had been gone through. There were papers and pens, paper clips, rubber bands and assorted desk junk all over the place. The two computers were still running. It appeared that the orange and blue screen-saver fish were the only witnesses to the double homicide.

The small plastic file that usually held dozens of 3.5 inch floppy disks, however, was missing, and so were the disks. I called to Toby.

"I'll note it," he said. "What was on them, their financials?"

"No. They ran the place from the computers next to the register. These computers were both Gil's." He was a programmer who was always working on something he claimed was revolu-tionary.

"I'll note that," Toby said and wrote on his pad. "I'll be talking to Stenopolis next, so we'll see if she has the disks."

Stenopolis is Alesandra Stenopolis. She and her husband Leo, owned the Red Dog and helped finance the Owen's computer business. She is the Grand Dame of Kootenai Falls, and I have never heard anyone refer to her in any way other than by her sur-name. She was not the kind of woman who elicited diminutives. She was a cross between Gertrude Stein and Marlon Brando — regally heavy, rigid, dominant, unapproachable, but otherwise charming. Stenopolis did not trust those who read books, and she despised any manner of sporting event. She drank Jack Daniel's beginning at ten a.m., and as far as I know no one has ever seen her fallingdown drunk. Elevated perhaps, but not drunk.

I was trying to avoid looking at Beth. The final insult was that terrible sight of her vulva, made worse by the arching of her back because of the tightening and solidifying of muscle tissue. (I noted that it is only after we vacate our bodies that non-medical people use the term *tissue*.)

"Can we maybe put something over her?" I asked.

Toby waved a yes and then asked, "Is that your dog yapping out there?"

It was indeed Jessie doing her complaining number. "She hates being excluded. Want me to shut her up?" I asked.

Toby shook his head no.

I had to get out of there anyway. Truth was that I had a fun *thing* for Beth, just as Roxy had said. A gentle flirtation. No harm done. Made us both feel younger than we looked.

Jess had stopped yapping when I walked past Toby and the highway patrol guys and said I'd check in later. She was in a sulky mood when I climbed into the driver's seat. She was lying on her side on her bed in the back. I always keep the back seats folded down so she has room to stretch out. This time she stared intently at the side of the truck, not looking at me. I guessed I was in the Red Dog too long. Or maybe I should have come out to see why Jessie was barking.

There may have been someone or other walking around near my car, or just where they shouldn't have been. That's known in our "family" as "Logic according to Jessie." She doesn't miss a thing, that girl. It's not easy being a father to a brilliant border collie. If Jess had been born human, she would have earned her Ph.D. at Harvard in something like astrophysics by the time she was twelve.

There was a scattering of something... pieces of something... to the side of the building. That might have been what Jess decided was worth barking at. I let her out just in case it was a pit-stop problem, and she ran right for the side of the store and began nosing into what I could now see were some kind of large feathers.

I called to Detective Wales. "You'd better take a look here," I said. "My dog's found something."

He came out, clipboard in hand, walked over and bent down. "I'll be damned. Looks like eagle feathers," he said.

Dennis, I thought immediately. Eagle feathers pointed directly to Indian involvement. In this case, without a moment's doubt, I knew Dennis was being set up. And as good a detective as Wales is, I was sure he would know it as well.

# John Herrmann

As for my relationship with Beth, we never did anything but flirt around, though we were both aware of the mutual attraction. It felt like a magnet was being passed over my hair and body when she was around. Once, though, she caught me alone in my office and hit me with a huge wet kiss. But I was Gil's friend as well, and she truly loved him. We both knew that. So there was never going to be anything but fun and friendship between us. Besides, I had my share of emotional drains before escaping to Kootenai Falls and I didn't need another complication in my life. Life is simple here, and I was firm about keeping it that way. I live alone with Jess in that log cabin with 41 llamas for neighbors and the nearest building is two acres away — a (luckily) failed Baptist church. I have about one acre, half of which is fenced perfectly for a few sheep so Jessie can sharpen up her trialing skills and keep in shape. I have my computer and modem and now, at long last and after much haranguing throughout the entire triple-murder investigation, I am on the Internet..., *finally*, my colleague at the paper had said. She had seriously coaxed me into the modern age. I also have my collection of CDs and cassette tapes of Vivaldi to sustain me through Montana winters. I have eleven versions of "The Four Seasons," and that is quite enough complication in my life. On the first warm day of spring you put on "The Four Seasons" and crank up the volume and go outside. That's what you do.

Other things, like a steamingly hot shower midday can help. And sometimes... nothing helps.

And of course there is Kate... always there will be Kate, who is still back there, surviving in New York.

With Kate every day was new. And now I see her perhaps once a year. I was thinking about her a few days ago when there was sun. It was early morning and so bright off the snow it blinded you. I was sitting at my pub table having my morning cup of Earl Grey and trying to ignore Jess' nagging about moving the sheep to the west pasture. Finally I saw it — a single strand of a web running down from the top corner of the window and connecting to the little basket a long-empty Chianti bottle was wrapped in. Once I saw it, I wondered how I could have missed it. In the thick early yellow light flashing through the window, the strand looked like a tiny rope. There was no clue to who had attached that line, but he or she was there — up there somewhere. And somewhere there was Kate, perhaps also in sunlight at this moment. Kate and I — we are attached by the thinnest of lines.

# Chapter Two

In a while, the reality of the violence came over me as I drove slowly, feeling my hands shake as they gripped the wheel. I drove in a kind of emotional haze back from the murder scene to the office. It was real then for me that Beth had been plunged into and both she and Gil had had their brains pushed out of their head by something like a small hammer going a thousand miles per hour. I felt it in my shoulders and my arms ached with it then.

I made a promise to myself — go home and work Jess on the sheep. There would be cleansing in working closely with her. She could be a hundred yards away and behind the sheep, but when our eyes met, we would each know what the other is thinking. I'd tilt my head to the right, she'd move right. Tilt left, and she moves... right — *if* she thinks the sheep should move that way. She is forgiving of human error, and as often as not, thinks for herself and does the work more efficiently for it.

I put the murder story into the computer while Jessie snoozed under my desk. When I finished, I sent it electronically to the copy desk and stood up, kicking Jess' water dish and slopping water over her front paws. She looked up at me then put her head back down and closed her eyes, presumably in disgust. As with most females, Jess is totally unforgiving of clumsiness.

I finally had something to write about, good, honest, personal stuff, like the brutal death of two good young people who had plans and opinions, dreams of going to Disneyworld someday, urges to go on the road on Harleys down to Mexico and maybe even Central America. They had grocery lists, and dentist appointments that now would have to be canceled by someone. They had reservations for dinner at the 44-MagnumSteak House just outside of town for their fourth wedding anniversary next Friday. Gil had ordered and had not yet picked up a set of cross country skis for Beth's anniversary present. And Beth was out of birth control pills and was about to talk with Gil about perhaps not buying more: "What do you think? We can afford a baby. I'm not getting any younger." And Gil was about to surprise her with his signed contract with a well known Seattle-based software manufacturer for the little thing he had been working on during those hot summer evenings last year. His programming ability, it turns out, was one of the important elements of this case.

I wrote a too-literary piece for Tom, but with that edge of strong feeling where small droplets of blood seep from your fingertips onto the keyboard:

*Gilbert Owen died late on a Saturday evening. As he entered the rear of the Red Dog Saloon that he and his wife, Beth, managed, along with a small electronics business, he saw his wife dead, nude, a smear of her blood on the wall behind her body. Her head was half missing, her legs were spread, her right arm was stretch out to the side.*

*Someone — a shadow — stood behind her.*

*Here is what happened: one bullet in the head for Beth Owen, one bullet in the head for her husband.*

*No time for understanding, to even put his hands up against the onrushing bullet.*

*That final image of his dead wife will travel with him. He is now only what he saw, and he will only be what he saw throughout clouds of formless nothingness, erasing the joy and substance of what Beth Owen had been, what he had been, what life, breathing, rain, sun had been.*

*Erasing everything.*

*Erasing all but the image of her, there, at the instant a droplet of brass-coated lead slammed into his skull at the forehead, exploding meat, bone, image, hope.*

# Chapter Three

I emailed Kate Wells at the Associated Press in New York City of what happened here. It wasn't much of a national story for her, but you never know. I like to give my friends all the support I can. News hounding is a very tough game at best. Journalists need friends to survive more than, say, dentists. Kate answered back quickly that I should explain, asking if there was an AP angle.

I picked up the phone and punched in those sadly familiar numerals. When I got her, she said in that quick big city manner, "What do you *mean* you have two murders in a saloon?"

"I mean — a couple who run a small saloon and computer business here were killed. She was raped and they were both shot. That's what I mean."

"Brewster, my love, that's not much of a story for me. Is that the only thing you have?"

"It was a reason to call you," I said. "Maybe what I'd like is that you might take some time off and come out and work this one out with me. Like old times," I said.

"Oh, so we'll work on a little guilt to get me out there?"

I said, "That's close." There was that hiss of distance between us. "If guilt will get you on the plane, I'll run through my usual litany."

Softly, she said, "I was talking with my friend Lenore last evening."

"And?"

"She said she'd always thought I moved in with the wrong man. That Ralph was just too — something else than what I am."

"Something else?"

"He's happy in his big job. He really buys into that executive status thing. He loves his lunches at those places you and I always avoided."

"Four Seasons, Twenty-One...."

She said in a tone that said she'd given up: "It's not that simple, Brew. He just doesn't understand. He can't imagine that ninety-thousand a year isn't the point. I have no way to make him understand."

"You know I can't tell you to leave him. You know that."

"I know that."

"But I can tell you to drop everything and fly out here and work up this very interesting story with me."

"Yes."

"I can do that," I said.

"Yes, you can do that."

I said, "So I'm doing that." I said, "I'm asking you to come out and stay with me, and this murder case will be our excuse to be together." I said, "Death and love, side by side."

"Sounds wonderful. But it's not an AP story."

"You could always quit," I said. "If you come out, I'll let you listen in when I call the FBI on this thing."

"Sweetheart," she said, "I work for the most impressive wire service in the world and you work for the least impressive bi-weekly in rural America. Who do you think they'll talk to when we both call? By the way, what's your circulation?"

"It's flirting with five thousand."

"I believe the AP has about a quarter of a million subscribing newspapers alone. That puts the readership at maybe two or three billion. So I bet I get better information than you do."

"Does that mean you're not coming out?"

She changed then. Her voice dropped. "I miss you so very much, Brewster."

"I miss some of your parts, Wells. I have a list here that doesn't include your brain."

"I love it when you talk sexist to me."

"The closest airport is about a hundred miles, over by Glacier. Tell me when."

"Don't do this to me."

"No, I don't mind. Really. I'll pick you up in Salt Lake, Denver... Kiev."

Silence then, and after a moment, she said, "I love you, Brewster. Any excuse like murder for us to get together is a good thing. But I really can't justify it now. But listen, here's something that you might want to work on," she said. "Look into something on the Net called Watchman. It's some kind of newsletter and information exchange from Montana somewhere, or maybe Idaho. Where's Sandpoint? Anyway, I'm not sure. It's very hard-core white supremacist stuff. There were exchanges of information about doing stuff in your area on the Net through this Watchman thing. Might be something there for your little community rag."

"Thanks for the tip. You usually don't share good stuff with me."

"Don't get used to it. I love you, Brew, but I'll beat your

ass any day of the week to a good story." She hung up.

Gone again. Damn but that woman never sits still long enough to get your arms around her. I held the receiver to my ear for a while listening to the empty sound. Kate was the best that ever came into my life. Now in her middle life she had it all together and needed to be in the thick of it where she could take advantage of the creative momentum in Manhattan. But commitment takes its toll. As for me, I am anti-complication, anti-relationship, and anti-anything else you can think of. Except, I missed the way she gasped.

# Chapter Four

"Gilbert was finishing with his special projects that were to bring him *ab...solute* wealth. *Enor... mous* wealth." Stenopolis rocked her thick body forward and stared into my eyes. "Wealth!" she said again in a whispered shout, her eyes swelling. Dennis O'Brien was with her in the living room, sitting quietly in a rocking chair across from where she was holding court. He always wore a kindly, and so far as I know permanent, smile. Something I now think is learned early by those minorities in our country who have been shown the value of subservience. It is an American heritage that our slaves and Indians smiled a lot to stay alive. Quoting from official U.S. policy circa 1800s: "A good Indian is a dead Indian... or a smiling, bowing, groveling Indian."

Stenopolis was the kind of woman who made each sentence into something Hamlet would say... to the back of the auditorium. She spoke in headlines. Her close-cut reddish hair just did fit around her head, plastered and unmoving at the sides and about her tiny ears. Those eyes — Poe would have described them as large and liquid. Eyes not made for seeing but for punctuation. At the close of a particularly meaningful line, they would swell wide as two hot-air balloons, commanding that you not look away, that you search into them, into her brain, for the earth-moving significance of her latest banal utterance. Her cheeks puffed as though Marlon Brando had shown her how to stuff cotton into them. Her lips were thin as dental floss. Below her chin was a mystery, as she was *wrapped* in cloth rather than dressed. She was the size of a post-menopausal mountain, draped in layers of silk shawls. Perhaps beneath the reds and greens, peacock blues and fringes there was a kind of muu-muu. No one I know has ever seen her feet.

But she was graceful; her wraps and shawls trailed on the carpet beneath and behind as she would glide like a ghost through the antique-cluttered living room. One could imagine tiny feet treading wickedly fast beneath her... so many hysterical toes trying to keep up.

Stenopolis is, at the same moment, elegant and ghastly.

She is in every detail the classic Greek broad, albeit one with an uncommon mind, as she was the first to tell you and to demonstrate. She often quoted Mark Twain, with minor modification, saying: "Leo [her husband] knows all that *can* be known..., and *I* know all the rest."

"You don't know about them?" she said, eyes rising, then narrowing into the sadness of my being left out of such things. "You see, he had worked for three years with Dennis here to eliminate, you know, that awful [pause], in*cred*ibly inane television advertising. It was an addition to the software in those little satellite dish things, you know, that some people buy."

"I didn't work much on that one," Dennis said, looking at his wristwatch, his long brown hair falling into his eyes. "I did some documenting for him, and he helped me with some code on another thing. That TV ad blocking program was easy. All he did was tie into that signal that networks always give — a bloop on the upper right or left-hand corner. That triggers an impulse. Gil just wrote a cut-out and cut-in then burned it into a chip and stuck it into a VCR. Simple. You start the VCR when the program begins, later you play it back without any commercials."

As a Stenopolis employee, Dennis did a bit of everything, including, but not exclusively, working in the back office, covering for the Owens, and doing a little programming on the side. He is light skinned Indian, tall, handsome, educated, as I have said, at the University of Montana. I never asked him what he was doing working for minimum wages in Kootenai Falls, and he never asked me why I was doing the same, probably because he knew I'd found my own version of nirvana. I think some of the problems he had around here stemmed from his being well educated. That isn't a thing a racist likes to see in a "non-white."

I asked Stenopolis for more details about the programming projects.

"Dear, I *have* no more details. But you may ask Dennis."

He stood, looked at his watch again. "Got to take care of that motor home clean-up. Anything else you have for me?"

"No, dear, run along. Tell Leo I said he needs to put a For Sale sign on the place for this weekend."

"I'll tell him." Looking at me, he said, "I might want to talk to you sometime about what Gil and I were working on."

"Whenever. Is it relevant to the murders?"

"Maybe," he said. "Who knows?"

"Right. Well, drop by the office, or maybe I'll see you at the Red Dog. You know about the evidence found at the crime scene?"

"The feathers? Yeah. Seems a little obvious that the killer would like to pin the crime on an Indian, doesn't it?"

"I doubt any detective would see it as more than a set-up. I wouldn't worry, Dennis."

"No," he said, "*You* wouldn't."

I asked about his girlfriend, Greta.

"On vacation," he said. "Over at the Swan for a while. She's pretty burned out. I told her to get away for a while or she'd fall apart."

The Swan is Swan Lake, some one-hundred miles southeast of Kootenai Falls. Greta Hahn was one of the few registered nurses who worked far too many hours at the small hospital in town. Overworked, underpaid is the rule in the medical professions everywhere, and more so in a small and poor community.

"When you talk to her, tell her to bring back a few fish and we'll have a breakfast together."

"I'll do it," Dennis said.

After he left, Stenopolis began describing what Gil was working on. "I know Dennis worked very close with him. And I... *permitted* it. On my time, you know. It was such a wonderful concept, how could I refuse?" Again, she rocked forward slightly, waiting to be appreciated. "There are few things in life worth more than eliminating television advertising. We would be nearing the perfect society. As you well know, Brewster, all evil derives from the sales pitch." Balloon eyes once again.

What were the other projects, I asked?

"One was quite secret, you know. Gilbert was brilliant with computers, and recently he had, you know, something to do with what they call *cyber*space." Her voice was husky, forced, giving away her awe at the new world of computers. "Several of these military types of people came by the office there to see him. I don't know what it was about except, as I say, *cyber*space." The emphasis was a signal for me to laugh and I accommodated her. "Gil was always working up things. He couldn't rest a minute." She pointed at the bank-like camera hovering above us on the ceiling near the doorway. "He was the sweetest boy, Brewster. He thought I should have *security*." The whites of her eyes blossomed once again. "And he kindly built me that contraption," she said, pointing.

Bob Able walked into the room. "I'm interrupting," he said. He is a tax attorney who once owned and operated the best fly-fishing store in the county. Able is a smallish but dapper businessman who is described by locals over beer at the Red Dog as a man with small hands, a big head, no heart, and the owner of the most expensive Mercedes in Montana. "It's worse than that," he says. "It's paid for!" Able gives occasional fly-fishing lessons at the baseball field in Kootenai Falls on Sundays — after church.

Stenopolis motioned for Able to sit down.

"I'll bet Bob is here with an offer to buy the Red Dog," I said.

Her face opened in surprise. "Yes, I suppose so," she said. "He's always wanted to open a museum in there."

"Oh, it's just a half notion," said Able. "I read about some pioneers out here who had an idea of building something new, something different from the way this country was going. I just wondered if there wouldn't be some artifacts and things — everyday things like an old American flag used by the army, or what have you — number one: that would be valuable and a good drawing card, and number two: to show how they lived and their intentions."

"You're not serious about a museum," I said.

Able laughed. "Only half. If I did do something like an offer here, I'd bring the Dog up to date technologically." He had the broad, icy smile of a man who owned every room he walked into. It was difficult to be around him, partly because of that constant toothy smile of his and his almighty arrogance. You might think of Bob Able as the antithesis of Dennis O'Brien. Word was that he is a closet white supremacist, but very deep into the back of that closet. It had never shown, as far as I know. But up here in the Northwest, it's easy to appear to be what is known as a bleeding heart liberal about blacks. Certainly most of the good people of Kootenai Falls welcome cultural diversity. But you occasionally find someone who will say, "We don't have a black problem here — we don't let them in." It happens in Chicago and it happens in small town America. The northwestern states have gotten their share of bad press about the militia movement and the nutty Aryan Nations trying to move in and cut away, secede from the rest of the U.S.

I asked Stenopolis if she were going to keep the Red Dog open.

"That will be up to Leo, but I think so. After this *horrible* thing, I don't ever want to *think* about that place again. How *dread*...ful." She stared, her eyes growing. "How ab...solutely... incomprehensible!" The eyes again, the rocking forward. And next to her, in the comfort of an overstuffed rocker, Bob Able grinned.

Then Stenopolis launched into one of her tirades about me living without a partner. I was youngish but not *so* youngish, I had plenty of money, I was not exactly repulsive to look at, so apparently I owed it to myself and to single women everywhere to "get with the program."

It was time for me to leave, and that is what I did. Outside, I passed Able's red convertible and wondered how he could be so insensitive. Unemployment is about twenty percent in Yaak County, although the newspaper and official word would deny it is that high. Driving around in a sixty-thousand dollar car had to be one of the most heartless things a businessman could do around here. "But look at it this way," he always said, "Number one: I pay good wages to a few kids to keep it polished. Number two: I encourage them to see how hard work and dreams can get you such a thing of beauty. Doesn't that help out?"

Twenty minutes after I got back to the office I had a visitor.

"Russell Pace, FBI," the man said, flipping his ID and badge at me. He was wearing a raw silk gray sports coat that was a little snug and had the large and pointed lapels one rarely sees these days outside of the major cities. We shook hands. "Can we talk here?" Pace asked.

I nodded.

"We're just talking to everyone on the list from the sheriff's office who had any contact with the crime scene. Can you tell me if you saw either victim alive within the last twenty-four hours?"

I said no but that I had seen Beth on Friday in this office.

"Was she alone?"

"Yes."

"How did she appear? I mean, did she seem anxious or worried?"

"I don't think so."

"What about any of the back room software projects?"

"I don't know of any," I lied.

"Wasn't it common knowledge that Mr. Owen was a programmer?"

"I suppose it was. But I don't pry into people's hobbies or businesses. I report on situations and incidents, game scores and church rummage sales, land slides, floods and the occasional student who is awarded a football scholarship."

"Well,' he said, "what will you write about this?"

I looked directly into his eyes and said, "You can read it in our Wednesday issue."

"I only meant...."

"I *know* what you meant. What I mean is that without a court order, no one reads what I write until the paper comes out."

"Look," said Pace, "We're on the same team. There's no sense getting combative."

"No sense at all," I agreed. "But you people know the rules. The rules are that I don't push you for information and you don't push me. For example, I haven't asked what the FBI is doing working simple homicides. You don't usually get involved in these kinds of things."

"We don't comment on ongoing investigations," Pace said.

"My point exactly. We don't give advance copies of our articles."

That was when Everett said, across his desk, "Don't get testy, Brew. We don't need an angry FBI around here."

"There's no danger of that," Pace said with a smirk. He seemed to me a man you do not trust alone with your dog. A handsome, albeit aging, "Ken doll" face you might see in an old black and white newsreel — a German tank commander in a starched khaki uniform at the Tunisian front, circa 1942.

Pace continued: "But it never hurts to ask, I always say. Some writers and editors are more cooperative than others...,"

"More cooperative?"

"... so we often just try it out. No problem." He pushed both palms toward me. "I doubt there would be anything in Mr. Moore's story that we don't already know."

I stood up. "More cooperative? You mean that playing by the rules and the laws of the land makes me *un*-cooperative?"

Pace reached over and patted my shoulder. "We're on the *same* team, Mr. Moore. I assure you *your* FBI does not wish to break any of your rules."

"*My* rules? *My* FBI?"

"But we have a serious situation here. I'm sure you want the investigation to go forward and be as complete as possible. So I do ask that if you come across anything that would be of value that you call us immediately." He handed me his card. "Call me any time. That's a beeper number."

After he left, Everett sighed and stood up. "Don't piss off the feds, Moore. That's the first rule of home town journalism. You're not in New York now, you're in Kootenai Falls, Montana.

The Bush, my friend. You survive in the Bush by not having ethics."

"That was incredible. Pace wouldn't last a week in a major city. I know for a fact they'd eat him up at the *Times*."

"The rules here are bendable. We bend them every day. I print stories about our local Chevy dealer's nine year old daughter going to summer Bible camp in return for his ads. I print stories about the great new sofas coming into Kootenai Falls Furniture and Appliance and accept their sixth-of-a-page ad for that issue. And I run the story on the page with the ad. That's the kind of business I'm running, Brew, and I do make mistakes sometimes. Like — I printed a bad review two years ago about a film that was showing here at our elderly movie theater, and we haven't gotten an inch of advertising from them since. The same is true with the feds. Play their game, writer, or your ass is hazel nuts."

Quietly, touching his forehead as if for emphasis, Everett said, "This is Kootenai Falls, this is not the world."

"I understand."

"I hope you do, son, because we can't take any tragic adherence to Ethics-in-Journalism 101 on the *Mountain Inquirer*. That may have been the ball game back in the States, as it were, but you're in the Bush now, Bubba."

Maybe he was right, I thought. Maybe all this is a game. Only when you're young do you take it seriously. And only a few, like Ben Bradlee, keep their adolescent sense of mission alive in their hearts to the end. I thought then that I would take myself off the story and write about the cougar overpopulation and the resulting threats to livestock and our children who walk to school in the darkness of an April morning. That would be a story of good and evil without a federal government angle.

I decided: at the right time, I would tell Tom Everett that Amy Kroll was perfect for the murder story. It would be her first big chance to put together a series and report it out and prove that she learned something in J-school. She had worked for five months keying in the "Sheriff's Report" each issue, and the obits., and church service listings. Maybe now it was time for her to look at murder.

"Do you think he was really FBI, Tom?" I sat back down and looked at Pace's card.

"He said he was. That's a big federal offense if he's not."

"Wouldn't be the first time."

"For what?"

"I don't know. I just have a feeling. I mean, why do I get a card without an address or phone number except for a beeper phone number?"

"He's on the road a lot? Hell, I don't know. He said FBI and I take him at face value. If he's not, that would not be your story to go after. I'm warning you, we do good mama and papa coverage here. We don't expose people posing as FBI."

"I think he's CIA. Did you see the size of his gun? No FBI agent I ever met walked around with a cannon like he had strapped under his arm, let alone running around far from home investigating a homicide. He also had a small automatic strapped to his ankle."

"You know, Brew, I'm worried about you. I wonder if you're cut out for this little paper. For one thing, it's not in your job description to take on the federal government. We do *local* stories, nice stories, sweet stories. Oh, we'll cover our mayhem as it occurs. Our readers expect it. But we cover it and let it go and let our readers re-bury their heads in the sand.

"Our main tone is not crime and punishment. We cover girl's fourth grade baseball and the local library's free Internet. We don't print stories about Bosnia or Oklahoma City. We don't print stories about child abuse, even when it's done here in town right on Main Street. And if we did, we'd be out of business in a New York second. You're a good guy to have around, Brew, and you work cheap. But this business is very different from the one you worked in back East."

"It's not so different. It's the same business, but the people running it there are different."

"Give it a rest, will you?"

I stood. "I'm not working here for the money. I don't need your $450-a-week handout. But you need good writing and honest reporting. Without a few of us around willing to work for the love of it, you wouldn't have a business at all, let alone any credibility. I could buy your pathetic newspaper out of what's in my checking account."

"It's not for sale."

"Oh? What about the Chevy dealer and the furniture store? No, Tom, I'd say this business is for sale — every day of the week."

Roxy came out of her office then and sailed between us. "Now then, boys, are we ready for a little drink? You've had enough exercise for one day."

I turned around to my desk and saw that Jess had slept through the whole disagreement. So much for dogs picking up on their master's emotions. Or maybe she's just heard it too many times before to pay much attention.

"How about the Red Dog?" she said. "I think they're open about now on Sunday... Unless they've closed it down. We could do the Sail Inn. But anyway, it sure sounds like you two are ready for the first drink of the day."

# Chapter Five

It was decided to keep the Red Dog open, but the rear entrance and the south side of the building was enclosed in yellow plastic crime-scene tape that had to be sent for, arriving from Spokane by currier. Kootenai Falls doesn't have enough serious crime to warrent keeping crime-scene tape on hand.

Tom, Roxy and I sat at the bar next to one of the locals. It would not be the Red Dog if you went in and Jim Letwilig wasn't sitting at the bar, a double Johnny Walker Red in front of him.

"Shit occurs," Jim Letwilig said. Big Jim is thick-bearded, six-foot seven, a gentle giant, one of four very tall Letwilig brothers — all with overgrown, bushy, mountain man beards — who live just a few miles up onto Lone Mountain, which is the first dirt logging road north of the Red Dog. It is a kind of militia playground, equipped with rifle range, and broken-down old army tank sans cannon, a jeep-like armored personnel carrier, and laundry hanging on the line always. And always with camouflage shirts and pants flying in the wind like jungle flags. I think all four Letwilig sons belonged, at one time, to the Montana Militia. Perhaps for different reasons. And I'm not sure any of them are dangerous, other than that they carried guns around with them in their various rattling vehicles. But hell, this is Montana: it's not a drivable pickup truck unless there is a rifle or .44 magnum riding along somewhere inside... in case you hit a deer and have to put it out of its misery.

Each Letwilig son has an acre or two with this or that broken down trailer and pieces of tin siding attached. Kellog Letwilig has a nice cedar frame over his doublewide, and that is the showplace of their little encampment. There is a handsome set of elk antlers attached to a log cross beam over the entrance to the property and the mandatory wagon wheels on either side, like an open gate, to let you know this home is populated by those who believe in a sentimental West and the honest and moral slaughter of sensitive animals known as "game." Of course, there is a flag-pole at the center of the compound with a carefully tattered American flag hanging down from the top in that tragic manner of a lost erection.

Kellog works occasionally as a hunting guide for an outfitter out of Noxon, an hour south of Kootenai Falls. It is said among the bars in town that someday there will be stories told far and wide about Kellog Letwilig's ability to find game for Jewish physicians from Greenwich, Connecticut, the way there are stories about Daniel Boone and the unfortunate bears who met up with him in Kentucky. One more thing: Letwilig has been a member in good standing of several paramilitary organizations. He describes himself, when you ask him, as a peaceful racist who doesn't despise "the Jew-controlled Congress and White House. I'm an anti-government activist, but I still pay my taxes," he says. "But there will come a day...." On some weekends, Kellog travels to Hiram Howell's property near Sandpoint, Idaho, where it is said that strong men train hard preparing to defend the American way of life.

Kellogg's brother Lamar works seasonally, they say. His live-in girlfriend, Suzanne Kellerman, teaches elementary school and gladly supports him when Lamar is between jobs. I say gladly because Lamar took pity on her after her fortieth birthday and asked her to marry him. At the time, he was just twenty-six. She moved in with him within the week, but so far, no wedding. That was three years ago. "I have tenure *and* Lamar," she says. "What more could a girl ask for?"

The youngest Letwilig son is nicknamed Shorty because he is just six feet tall. Shorty Letwilig joined the navy on his eighteenth birthday, during his third run at the tenth grade. He was stationed at Miramar Naval Air Base near San Diego, but the last anyone heard from him was in 1996 from a Mexican jail in Baja where I have heard he is serving life for trying to buy an ounce of maryjane. No Letwilig has yet bothered to drive down and see exactly what is going on. They all start in on the beer too early to do much planning on any given evening. But I suspect when they do get a plan developed, they will go down in their armored personnel carrier equipped to "argue" with the Mexican police and army. Jim told me once that he thought Shorty was just dodging some girl he knocked up, that he wasn't in jail and that no jail, especially a Mexican jail, could hold him for very long anyway. However, it seemed to me that two years in a Mexican jail is a very long time.

Big Jim, who occasionally accompanies Kellog over to Howell's gatherings at Sandpoint, is the eldest of the four, lives in a 1930s-era fourteen-foot silver camper trailer set up on cement blocks. Inside, the trailer is neat, with everything put away. He claims to be orderly to a fault. Still, he says, "no woman would have me." Whenever you go into his tiny trailer, you see nothing out of place. All the counters are cleared with maybe only a recent *Hustler* on a table top, perhaps meant as proof that Jim can read. There is never any clutter. No laundry to be done or put away, and no food-crusted dishes in the sink. Outside, though, it is another story. Jim has every tire that ever came off any of the Letwilig brothers' cars stacked on the north side of his little fortress. He also keeps a small pink pig and four or five chickens. "I keep the chickens so I'll have something to kick when I'm in the mood. I also have them so the pig has something to eat if I come home late," he says. "The pig eats the eggs, the shells, and if I'm real late he'll eat a chicken, feet and all."

You wouldn't like Jim if you met him. But Montana is not Manhattan, and Jim seems to me to maintain a reasonable balance between having good heart and carrying a .357 magnum. I like him despite his ferocious anti-government attitude. And if you ever get into a bad fight at the Red Dog, or in town at the Eagle's Club or the VFW, it's Big Jim Letwilig who will get you out of it. He did that for me once. At my age I am no barroom brawler. When I was young, I was even less of a fighter. So when a guy who was working with control burning gangs around the mountains started picking on me, Jim stepped between us and smiled at the guy, then reached down and took hold of his balls. He talked slowly as he squeezed and the guy, doubled over as he was, kept yelling to let go. Jim let go and stood back then and said in that even and quiet Western manner that the guy could leave now and that the only bar in town he should stay out of was the Red Dog Saloon. I never saw the guy again.

"Shit occurs," Jim was saying. "But this kind of shit usually doesn't happen in Montana. It's reserved for the streets of Detroit."

Tom emptied his mug of Moose Drool before I even touched mine. "That stuff'll kill you," Big Jim said. "How can you do that to yourself?"

Tom didn't acknowledge Jim's presence, let alone anything he might say. But Roxy looked up at Big Jim and then at his drink. "I suppose that's your Johnny Walker Red."

"It *is* that," he said.

"And that's better for you than beer, I suppose."

"Yes, ma'm. It gets me drunk quicker with less liquid, therefore I find it the superior drink." He smiled and touched the brim of his black baseball cap. "What's that you're drinking?" he asked her.

"It's called a dirty white boy."

Unsmiling, Jim said, "Don't put one o' them in your mouth, you might get pregnant." It was said with grace, in that straight-faced Western manner that can be taken as friendly, no matter the words.

"If you want to know what I think," Jim said, "I think it was those storm trooper types killed them people."

"Neo-Nazis is what they call them today, Jim," I said.

"Whatever." He played with his glass thoughtfully. "You ever see their crap on the Internet?"

Tom looked over. "Do you read that stuff, Letwilig? I knew you were an asshole, but I didn't think you were a *complete* asshole."

Ignoring him, Jim said to me, "You ought to give it a try. There's nuts everywhere, but there's some common sense stuff comes from some. It's called Troopers and you can get on the list free to see for yourself."

I held back on a confession that I had no Net experience beyond simple e-mail. Actually, I had tried it once here in Kootenai Falls, doing a story about its library putting in an Internet server for the community. But I was fearful of damaging the equipment and threw my hands up in the air first chance I got.

"Don't you still belong to that bunch?" Tom asked. It was Tom-the-reporter now. He put his question in that flat news hound manner one uses while looking down, taking notes.

"The Militia isn't like that. Most we ever do is go turkey hunting together."

"I see," said Tom. "You don't plan to overthrow the government by force."

"Some do, some don't."

"And you?"

"I don't hang out with crazies and I'm not one myself. But I like my guns the way you like your computers." He smiled to himself on that line and pushed his empty glass across the bar which, at the Red Dog, is the equivalent of politely asking the bar maid for another Johnny Walker Red, please.

Tom put away another Moose Drool and I said he'd been in a nifty mood all day. "Is this your Sunday attitude?" I asked.

He also pushed his glass across the bar. "I read a review of a book of stories by a friend of mine in the *Times*. That did it. That and two murders can ruin a who day."

"Crucified him, did it?"

"It was the best rave review I've read in a while. He called the book 'beautiful.' Said it had grace. It's supposed to be about happy love that sweetens complicated lives."

"And that's why you're in such a lousy mood, because your friend got a rave review?"

He looked across the bar at the bottles. "I'm usually not a competitive man, but I hate it when my friends do things I can't do."

"That's what I call mean-spirited."

"I like that expression." His smile was the smile of a possum eating dog shit. "Has a nice ring to it. *Mean-spirited*," he said, trying it out. "Yeah, I like that. I think I'd like to live up to that phrase." His eyes narrowed then at the bar girl, but he kept his shit-eating grin. "Hit me again, Sally," he said, both elbows out on the bar now like a broken hawk.

"Well," I said, "while you're in this mean-spirited mood, what about discussing taking me off the homicide story and putting Amy on it? I have a couple of features going that will satisfy your need for happy and innocuous copy, and Amy has enough experience now to do a great job on her first really important story."

"Bull shit."

"She'll get along with the CIA better than I do."

"FBI, not CIA."

"She's sweet and good-looking, and all steel inside. That's a great combination for a reporter."

"No."

"I'll call her right now and tell her she's on the story."

"She's not on the story. Don't lie to the girl."

"I'll be right back."

"If you call her and tell her she's on the story, call yourself and tell yourself you're fired."

"I only have one quarter."

"There's always a simple solution, Moore. If you only have one quarter, what do you do? You call Amy and tell her she's on the homicide story, then you tell her to call you and tell you you're fired."

Big Jim was listening closely, looking straight across the bar and frowning.

Roxy stood up from her stool on the other side of Jim and walked up to Tom. "Don't be an asshole, Tom. Give the man a quarter."

# Chapter Six

As it worked out, I did call Amy to tell her that the two of us were assigned to the homicide story and that I would pick her up at her house at nine the next morning and we would start looking into things more closely.

I also called Kate Wells for a source check. "Can you get me someone who would know about this FBI person. Or whoever he works for?"

"There's a former agency guy in Denver who helps us now and then. His name is Michael Solo." She gave me the number. "He may talk, then again he may not be in the mood. He's not a consistent source. And," she said, "don't burn this guy. He's one in a million."

On my way to pick up Amy on what was the last Monday in April, I swung around the corner of Sixth and Seeley and met a white van speeding along, headed directly at me. It was icy and there was hardly enough room for us to pass one another even if the van were on its own side, which it was not. I slid up almost effortlessly onto the sidewalk, missing a tree and a lamp post as the van continued on its way as though I did not exist. I unbuckled my seatbelt and got out to figure how best to get back onto the street when a small voice from behind said, "You were lucky."

Turning, I saw a man possibly in his eighth decade, with cane, grinning at me. "Last one got totaled."

"The last one?"

"That was old Hiram Howell. Thinks he owns the road. He totaled my neighbor's white Bronco couple weeks ago."

"The asshole went through a stop sign," I said, assuming this old man had missed that important element.

"He owns them too. Makes the law here on Seeley Street. Best you remember that. It's a good thing you aren't a black man."

"He doesn't like blacks?" I asked.

"He don't make a secret about whatever he thinks," the old man said. He turned and started back toward his house. "Best to go down Utah or Louisiana streets this time o' day."

"Thanks for the advice."

"Utah's best. He don't own nothin' on Utah."

"Who's Hiram Howell?" I asked Amy after she got into the car.

"He owns Seeley Street," she said.

"He tried to run me over a few minutes ago."

"That's because you were on his street. I heard he emigrated here from Europe and got rich on real estate deals. A real racist asshole is what I've heard. He owns land over in Idaho where a bunch of the militia types meet and play war on weekends."

"Yeah, some old guy back there told me he had a thing about blacks. But why does he own a whole city street? Who owns streets? They belong to the city. We *all* own the streets."

"All of them, except Hiram Howell owns Seeley," she said, laughing. "Just accept some things, Brew, or you'll end up antagonizing everyone and your fenders will look funny. Anyway, Hiram is a self-appointed Colonel. That's how some of the camo guys refer to him."

"Oh, I see. He owns a city street *and* an army. Is he one of those funny boys. Is he going to get even for Ruby Ridge?"

"Not exactly. He'd probably be in the background funding a private enterprise. It'll be fun watching him. You'll get a kick out of how serious they take themselves. But it's best to stay off his street. Paranoids are good at coming up with reasons to add names to their enemies lists."

Howell, it turns out, was a former history teacher in a gymnasium in Amsterdam who came to the U.S. after Germany surrendered. Until he retired a decade ago, Howell operated a successful real estate business in Yaak County and personally bought up many of the smaller homes on the northeast side of Kootenai Falls including fifteen or so on Seeley. He grabbed some two-hundred acres near Sandpoint, Idaho and put a few barrels full of dollars into military style fencing. Some time back he hosted a weekend convention with *Soldier of Fortune* magazine writers and editors, and some strange minister from Arkansas came up and talked about getting God back into white America.

Talk in Kootenai Falls of Hiram's aggressive driving habits included the advice to get off the roads when Hiram got into his white van. One thing about him — he dressed to kill always. They say you never saw Hiram outside of his small house without a severely pressed and starched white dress shirt, open at the collar, and always in summer the same white gabardine sports coat over a pair of neatly pressed slacks. Except for the Bob Ables of this world — obsessively natty dressers who would be uncomfortable without their business suits or Harris tweed jackets — the uniform of the day (and night) in Kootenai Falls is, and will always be, a baseball cap, T-shirt and jeans and, in winter, sweatshirt, jeans, parka and hightop boots. They say around town that one reason Hiram likes to dress up all the time is he loves the lady nurses and always hangs out with them.

Hiram was one exception in dress. Still very European. Also in his politics that reflected the 1930s mood, as he obviously sided with the white supremacists. But as far as I could tell, he'd kept that pretty much to himself. He had few friends, except the nurses from the local hospital and nursing home. He was known as a serious, albeit old, flirt. Apparently with a starched white shirt and jacket, he was not a disgusting dirty old man.

It was snowing lightly, a late winter wet snow, when Amy and I got to the office behind the Red Dog. Detective Wales and the CIA/FBI fellow, Pace, were standing just inside the yellow crime scene tape. I let Amy out and sat behind the wheel and waited. I couldn't hear them but could tell from Toby's body language that Amy wasn't getting anywhere. When she came back she said there would be a press conference at eleven a.m. and that we'd have to wait until then for an update.

"One newspaper in town and we're having a press conference?"

"Looks like the others are coming in today," she said. "The *Missoulian*, for one."

"If they can get in. I hear it's snowing pretty hard south and east of us." I opened my door then. "I want to check something," I said.

Wales nodded as I approached. I walked past the crime scene tape and to the side of the building where Jess had found what looked like feathers. Apparently Wales had picked it all up and the snow was now brushed flat and clean of debris.

"Was it eagle feathers?" I asked.

Wales nodded then stared at me with that "you're bothering me, can't you see I'm busy with important matters" look.

I went back to my car and Amy and I drove up to the Kootenai Falls Cafe´ then.

"Had breakfast?" I asked Amy.

"No, I don't eat breakfast. I'll have tea with you, though."

Inside, the place was nearly empty. We took a table by the window. "So — what do you think?" I asked. I ordered my usual suicidal breakfast of four link sausages and two sunnyside-up eggs, dripping hash browns and white toast. I also take half-and-half in my coffee. My philosophy says that there is nothing sexier than sausage breath.

"I have no idea. I'm completely mystified."

"That's because you're supposed to be. Usually, a murder has a couple of obvious motives and one or two obvious suspects along with three or four obvious pieces of evidence that links it all together."

"Well, there is a motive in what Gil was working on."

"That's right," I said. "And that's where everyone is looking. And as far as the cops go, they have to look there. And it took twenty-four hours for them to get to it. But that's their job. Our job is different."

"So, where do we look?"

"We use our peripheral vision. We look at the murders and we look at the kind of people the victims were. I guess. Hell, if I knew, I'd be sheriff. I know one thing — what you do is take the time of the murder and try to move backwards in time with the victims through the hours before their deaths."

"The most obvious thing is that murders are related."

"And in that connection there must be some revealing thing. Some giveaway."

"There is?"

"There has to be. Or else the homicides aren't related. Even by chance. For instance, the simplest: *he* was killed because he was there when *she* was killed. That's the easiest link, and maybe the one the killer wants us to believe. But we don't know what the real connection is yet. All we know is that there will be something that will point at motive and killer. The sexual assault has to be accounted for as well. And eagle feathers."

Amy frowned. "That's a pretty clumsy set-up of the Indian guy."

"Always fun to get the Indian," I said. "But setting down a few feathers might point more to the real killer than Dennis O'Brien. All I hope is that our beloved prosecutor thinks the same way.

"Another thing," I said, "why are the federales in on this? I'll tell you why. It's because there was something going on *before* the crimes. The FBI doesn't get into the act on mere homicide. Serial murder, yes. But there's nothing on the surface here to indicate an FBI investigation. Also, Agent Pace arrived here mere hours after the bodies were found— here in this remote location, a hundred miles from an honest-to-god airport. I say the FBI was here all along, maybe doing something else, and only coincidentally were around when the murders where committed. They've been working on something here, whatever it is, a lot longer than two days."

"They?"

"FBI agents don't work alone. I'll bet you that Pace has a partner somewhere in the woodwork. It could be as routine as tracking down the militia guys on something."

The eggs, sausage, toast and potatoes came, all on an oval hubcap-size plate. Rita, who served me at this cafe´ no matter where I sat, looked down at me with her smile. But it was her dancing eyes that always made me unable to speak. But a woman that gorgeous is not someone waiting around for an older aging newspaper reporter to ask her out.

A beautiful smile, one that could easily break your heart. Her eyes stab and hold you along with her smile. She had satin hair and eyes made for squinting into darkness — all merging with a childlike beauty I had always thought was wasted on the old farts who hung around here over their coffee watching her *be*hind move. "Anything else, cutie?" she asked. There is hidden elegance in this woman, and all it would take is a few beers with her at the Red Dog some sweet, cool summer evening for me to bring it out. ("Avoid complication," Jiminy Cricket whispered into my left ear.)

"Yeah," I said. "Punch my card." To Amy I said, "You buy a hundred high-fat meals in here and when your card is completely punched full of holes, they give you a free rosewood coffin."

"For another fifty breakfasts, we throw in satin lining and an AM/FM portable radio with longlife batteries," Rita said.

"I hate the music you play in here. I'll hate it even when I'm dead."

"But if you're going to be in the ground, maybe it's a comfort to have the weather report," Rita said. She smiled and swished away with a coy look.

"What's the deal with that dog of yours?" she asked. "You seem really married to her."

"It's a long story."

"What's the short version? She's really beautiful."

"She was this farm dog of a friend of mine who died. I passed through when I came here from New York to visit his widow and saw this gorgeous border collie out under a tree not moving. She was in mourning, deep depression."

"So you picked her up and made her well again?"

"No," I said. "I just asked my friend's wife about her, and

then drove away, down the dirt road to the main gate. I made the mistake of checking in the rearview mirror and saw the dog on the porch looking after me. She hadn't moved from her spot by the tree waiting for her master to come home for almost a year." It was hard talking about it, but I managed to tell her I went back for Jessie and we'd been friends ever since.

"I never had a friend like that," Amy said. She looked down at her hands. Then, as an afterthought, she said, "I've heard a lot of rumors about you."

"I'm sorry about that. It happens if you come here from a big city."

"I heard you had a tragedy happen to you."

I said nothing.

"That you were married once when you were a lot younger."

"I know what you're getting at and I'd just as soon...."

"That your wife went off and killed herself."

I let it ring in the air around us for a moment, then I looked at her and said, "It was a tragedy, yes. But it is her tragedy, not mine. She's been dead now for almost twenty years."

"You never let on about things like that," Amy said, her thin smile trembling the corners of her mouth.

"No — and you don't either," I said.

I changed subjects because it was time. "Do you speak Internet?"

She straightened her shoulders then and answered, "We used it a lot for research in J-School. Why?"

I explained about Troopers and that Watchman thing Kate had mentioned; I said I wanted to find out firsthand what they were thinking.

"You subscribe to lists, if you want to. It's not the usual kind of subscription. You don't pay. Then you get e-mail messages forwarded from the list host. Are you following?"

I nodded weakly. Outside, the snow had stopped falling. It's hard not to be more interested in the weather than the Internet.

"It's a kind of open dialogue, and all the messages that come in go out to everyone on the list."

"So why haven't you pushed for a connection at the paper?"

"I'm a newbie, remember? Newbies don't ask for modems and things like that."

I asked Amy then about why she came to work at such a low-keyed rag of a paper. "I'm curious about why a person would spend four years getting a journalism degree and then end up in

Kootenai Falls."

"First of all, I haven't *ended up* anywhere yet. I'm originally from San Francisco, and I've gotten two kinds of questions about that. One is: 'How could you ever leave a city like San Francisco?' I tell them I hate cities and couldn't wait to get out."

I didn't tell her I was from Oakland. No one needs to know things like that after you've managed to get away.

"Is that true?"

"No. But people don't expect the truth when they ask stupid questions like that. The other thing I get all the time is: 'Have you lived in Kootenai Falls all your life?' I tell them — 'Not yet.'"

"But why Kootenai Falls?" I asked.

"I get lost in cities... emotionally. I found that out when I interned back East. I don't recognize myself. It's funny. I don't have words to describe the feeling. But I just feel like I'm living inside this body, being pulled around from event to event. I don't feel that way here so much. Here, I feel connected to myself. But I still feel a little like I'm trapped inside this body playing a role.

"I imagine sometimes that I'm a puppet," she said. "I fantasized about that when I was little. I walked around stiff and smiling pretty, and when my mother would ask what I was doing, I would slump forward and say I wasn't doing anything. I was afraid to tell her that her daughter was a puppet."

"Big cities will do that to you," I told her. "I didn't feel like a puppet in New York, but I was one. That's a big difference."

"That's big city stuff. Everyone is part of a machine and they know it. This thing with me was different." She leaned toward me. "When my boyfriend and I slept together, I really, really thought someone was pulling strings on my arms and legs. I never told anybody this ever, but... I never felt a thing. I acted pretty good, but I couldn't feel him." She searched into my eyes as if I might have an answer for her.

I wished then that I knew her well enough to say things that you can only say to those who you love. "And now? I mean, are you seeing anyone now... you know...?"

"I'm afraid to test it here. So I haven't met anyone."

"Not in four months? At your age?"

"What's age got to do with it?"

I would have liked to bring back those words, but I said, "You're in your mid-twenties, right?"

"Right on the button. I'm twenty-six."

"That's primetime for a woman. I'd imagine that...."

"Maybe we ought to get going. I'm feeling pushed."

"I'm not pushing. Anyway, maybe your boyfriend didn't

have much for you to feel. Why do women always, *always*, think that whatever happens is their fault?"

"Well, I'm feeling pushed right now. I shouldn't, I know. But let's get going."

"Good," I said. "I've made you feel."

I knew how good that line was because I saw the reddish color come to her cheeks. It might have been anger, it might have been embarrassment. But she felt something strong enough to change the color of her skin. I was a tad better than the boyfriend, even at my white-bearded age. There is definitely something to be said for middle age where experience, judgment and strength of character come together. You think that way and, all of a sudden, that asshole Jiminy Cricket appears. "Don't even *think* it," Jiminy screams. Okay, okay, I say. I know. I know.... Walk on by.

After breakfast, I called in to see how Jess was doing under my desk without me. The lines were all busy so I hung up and walked with Amy over to the courthouse, making sure our arms didn't touch accidentally and cause Jiminy to hemorrhage. I didn't want to send a wrong message to her and, as a result, possibly complicate my naturally beautifully simplified life of no love and no human contact, let alone piss off that Cricket.

We went into the big room where town meetings were held and where the press conference was scheduled.

"It's off," said the woman who works the counter of the revenue office.

"It is?" Amy asked.

"They found another body," the woman said.

# Chapter Seven

This time I didn't look. I'd heard enough between the grumbles and police talk to understand that I didn't want to see this, also a single bullet to the head. From a distance.

It was the same caliber used to killed Beth and Gil, same (or similar) feathers found outside.

Because of the location, the body was mis-identified at first as Dennis' friend, Nurse Greta. Of course, no one in the sheriff's department would allow a boyfriend, especially an Indian, to identify a corpse. A few other people came around to help, but the official word from the police was that only close relatives would be allowed to see and identify the body. But when Greta showed up for work for her 11:00 P.M. shift straight from her weekend at the Swan, the Sheriff's Department had to scramble.

Things such as fingerprinting victims and dental ID-ing are not generally done in the first-hours of investigative procedure of a small town sheriff's department, because most everyone knows everyone else. Oh, it would have eventually been done. It was merely an oversight at the moment not to have properly ID-ed the victim. Which begins to explain for me why the FBI is in on this.

It was enough to make me head back to the cabin for a hot shower and let Jessie take the sheep from one field to the other. Or just harass the hell out of them. I felt like harassing something. Murder can affect you that way.

I settled for a cool shower and a beer.


The victim was mid-forties, approximately the same age as Greta, with the same mouse-colored dirt-brown hair and slim frame. The difference was that the victim was pregnant, recently divorced, and her ex-husband was a sometime Texas-style guitar player in the saloons in Kootenai Falls and Elk City. His name was Arnie Williams and he claimed to be a cousin of Hank Williams, Jr., who lived part of the year down south of Missoula in the Bitter-root.

# MURDER AT THE RED DOG

After searching the police bulletins for recent missing persons and finding nothing, the ex-husband eventually waltzed into the sheriff's office to say that his ex-wife had called him several days before to say she'd be by in an hour or so. Sixty hours had passed since that time. Arnie said that he was on the *threshold* of *beginning* to *start* to *initiate* some amount of worry about her.

"This ain't like Gidge," he said. Gidge was his pet name for her. Her real name was Lynette Okla, which one would think is a name that doesn't require anything additional. She had stopped using her husband's surname after their divorce, though I searched and could find no legal action that would have restored Okla to her.

Amy told me you could have slid a small tangerine into the exit hole on the right side of her head.

Arnie said with no emotion, when they pulled back the sheet in the morgue, "That's Gidge. Whatinhell happened here?"

I wrote that down just as it happened because it was hard to believe. It would not be in any story I wrote. Nevertheless, I wrote it down. When I did and when I closed my notebook, a chill went up the back of my neck and into my hair. I was either hungry for a Red Dog pizza, or else I was due for a "Sports Therapy" full body massage at Ginnie's just up the road from my place.

Either one would do.

Or both.


"Why kill her at Greta's?" Bob Able asked, his hands in his hair. There was a gathering of police, news hounds and local businessmen and women outside of the Kootenai Falls public library on Eli and 10th Street, next door to the Court House that also housed the sheriff's office. Among them, Able, Detective Wales, Leo Stenopolis and Lamar Letwilig, newly clean shaven, wearing a white T-shirt that was painfully clean, and looking as though he might have gotten an office job.

The day had warmed, much to the displeasure of the few local skiers who would have to keep an eye out for snow slides. But standing outside in the direct sun was a pleasure none of us had experienced for over a month. Of course, Able's shining red Mercedes was parked right where everyone had to trip over it... in the sheriff's personal space. A red $60,000 car, a $125 silk tie and another new pair of eye glasses designed for attending the Academy Awards ceremony are really a requirement for a youngish

Kootenai Falls tax attorney on the way up. However, no one was complaining. That's what money will do for you in a little town. Old Hiram Howell's white van was parked in the lot as well, but I didn't see him among the group. I was told that you can't miss him, that he walks like a marching gorilla, arms swinging freely and a huge gait with his head rotating side to side with each step. Ah, but always within his starched white dress shirt and white gabardine coat. Slicked-back thinning white hair, dark eyebrows and thin-line mustache, and a European arrogance. One thinks of an older Major Heinrich Strasse of *Casablanca* in civilian clothes, striding along like a handsome, well turned-out primate.

"To misdirect." someone answered. "Gain time."

"I don't think so," I said. "I think she was killed there because she was there. The killer wanted to kill *someone* in that house. It wasn't an interrupted robbery, seems to me."

To kill at a location regardless of who the victim is? That's reasoning too strange for a policeman's mind. Wales talked over me: "I have to look again at the crime scene."

I asked him about the feathers outside of the house.
"Again, probably some kind of Indian ritual, but it could be a pretty crude set-up. There were peyote pieces this time as well."

"Religious?"

"I wish I knew. That FBI agent, Russell Pace, he called into the Washington office and had them research it. Peyote is used over in Browning sometimes by the Blackfeet and down on the Flathead reservation. It's just the kids though; it's not used in any official religious way. And it's grown in the Southwest, in New Mexico and Arizona and across the border in Mexico. And Hopis use golden eagle feathers in some of their religious doings."

A voice from the back of the group yelled, "We don't need theories, we need an arrest!"

Nevertheless, theories were growing every which way.

"I'm not supposed to tell you this," Toby said, "but the results came back on the autopsy on Beth. They didn't find any semen in her. No male fluid traces at all. No pubic hairs besides her own. Nothing like you'd expect in a rape case. They also think she was dead before she was penetrated."

I shook off the ugliness of that. "So have you discussed motives yet?" I asked.

"Yeah, but now it's up for grabs again after this one."

"I didn't look, Toby. Was this Lynette person penetrated?"

"As far as we can tell now, no. We can't be sure until the forensic guys show up and do their number. But she had all her clothes on." He stopped then and put his hand on my shoulder.

"You're not writing any of this up in the paper are you?"

I assured him that Kootenai Falls readers had no interest in these details until they came from an official source, then and only then we'd print them.

I was wrong. When I got back to the office, Amy was at work on the new developments in the story, along with everything she had overheard at the scene.

"That's violating a trust," I told her.

"I didn't agree to anything, you did. If I overheard you two, then that's the detective's problem, not mine." She kept on working at the Mac as we talked.

"My agreement was for the paper as well as for me. You can't break that."

She stopped typing and looked down at her hands. "Shit. Shit shit shit shit shit! I get a handle on a breaking story and you guys take it away from me."

"This is the real world, Amy. Give and take is what we do to earn a living off information. The game has its rules." Under my desk, Jess gave me a sidewise fisheye glance. It was time for a workout. As I followed her to the door, Amy looked up. "Dinner tonight?"

I turned and silently put my hands out, palms upward.

"Not that kind of dinner, you dirty old man. Do you have a modem at home?"

I said I did.

"And some communication software?"

"Yes. Remember I get e-mail."

"Then I'm coming over with a Net browser and we're going to do some Web surfing. I'll be mentor to the mentor and bring you up to the twentieth century."

# Chapter Eight

Before moving the sheep to a fresh pasture, I settled down on the deck with a mug of Darjeeling tea, as I had read Horace Rumpole does. I had been reading stories of Rumpole of the Bailey, who often settles in with a cup of Darjeeling, which seems to me so literate and civilized, British and non-Montanan. What you're supposed to have on a deck in the sun of an afternoon near the Yaak is a longneck bottle of Moose Drool. Black Star at the least. Also, unlike Rumpole, I congratulated myself on not having anyone around by the name of "She Who Must Be Obeyed," otherwise known as Hilda Rumpole.

I did have a marriage, years ago, but I got over it. My "ex-" was someone like Roxy Everett who could find cause for argument over the immorality of wearing white before Easter.

But finally Jessie couldn't stand it any longer and was pacing about and whimpering. So I fetched my shepherd's crook and followed her to the gate at my east meadow.

I opened the gate and told her to wait while spreading the gate's wings back all the way. The sheep's heads were up, and as soon as I uttered "come bye," the dog leapt out clockwise and the sheep moved together to my right, away from the dog's pear-shaped outrun toward them. Jess swung to the middle of the field, stopping and turning them. I backed through the open gate, and Jess saw where I was going and continued a wide circle to the right, looking straight ahead and not at the sheep, her averted glance taking stress off of them. They settled and came forward then, turning down toward me until they were exactly between me and the dog. Jess stood still until they had gotten almost to me and then stepped forward one step to urge them on. As they began to think of scattering, perhaps turning back, she corrected, weaving back and forth, her body tilted forward, head low, rump high, eyeing the sheep over her lowered muzzle. At the slightest indication that they would bolt, she dropped like a rock. Then, when the sheep had time to think about what few alternatives they had, she rose butt first and took a another single step forward, and sheep gave up and ran past me through the gate and into the west pasture, Jess following quickly. I told her, "That'll do," and she lay down at the fence line and I closed the gate and told her what a good girl she was.

I went back to my Darjeeling and Jess sat with me in the sun and watched over our flock of three. I may not know anything about Internets, but I know that the reason border collies can weave behind sheep, correcting and driving them forward, is because after being sheared, sheep have 320 degree vision. Therefore, with very little head movement, sheep can see what's behind them. That coupled with a border collie's superior vision — they can see sheep a half-mile away — makes for an effective working combination. Unlike that of Amy-the-Internet-teacher and Brew Moore the cyberspace moron.

"You can't hurt anything," Amy said, hands on her hips, standing over me like an angry piano teacher. Dinner was going to be pizza and pitchers of Moose Drool Brown Ale at the Red Dog. But it was to be my reward for whatever successes I would have in... *cyber*space, as Stenopolis would say.

Jessie was right underfoot and wouldn't move away. She had a *thing* for Amy and there was no denying Jess the extended scratching and cooing-over that Amy gave her. Amy just abandoned trying to talk to me at first, got down on the carpet and romped with Jess, whose smile was as broad as I've ever seen it — teeth menacingly white, pink tongue out a foot long, and her eyes crinkling with delight at being the center of Amy's world, even for a moment. In the middle of being rubbed hard and kissed persistently on the top of her white muzzle, Jess pulled her head back and closed her mouth, looked very serious, then leaned toward Amy and barked once, loudly, in her face. Then Jess pulled back and out came that border collie smile again.

Finally, Amy rose and we went back to work. She directed me through the motions of calling up the local host server using her account then bringing up the software she installed for getting around. That got me to the Internet and searching the Web for racism, nazis, white supremacists. I finally came up with a listing that included "Trooper-L" and called it up.

After reading the junk on its home page about how the Jews have taken over and the traitorous liberal judges and other officials have sold out white America, I found other linked sources listed. Among them, something called the National Alliance and many other such names for organizations dedicated to returning

America to a white, Christian society... by whatever means.

"I'm convinced," I said and pledged to research on the Internet whenever I could.

After we disconnected I poured two small glasses of Courvoisier.

"I'd heard about all this," I said. "But reading it first-hand gets to the gut."

"Wait till you hit the porno stuff. Some of it even makes *me* blush."

"Indeed, and you're such a hard crusty little thing."

"I think this white supremacist stuff really took off on the Internet after Waco. Then came Oklahoma City and there was a clear them-versus-us dialogue." There was a world of connective illness just waiting there beneath our fingertips. Stuff there that Hitler's boys wouldn't have dared broadcast. As we got into wondering what we journalists should be doing about what was happening, the phone rang. I let the answering machine take it. It was Kate in New York wondering how I was doing.

At the Red Dog we ordered a combo pizza with whatever the cook had too much of. The brown ale was thick and bitter, good against the night chill, and later, by July, would be good against the thin and dry summer mountain heat.

We toasted to the dangerous mix of cognac and draught beer and then I told her I would interview Dennis O'Brien in the morning. "I think he's in a tough spot, if he doesn't have an alibi," I said. "I'll be interested in his perspective and who he thinks the killers are."

"Plural?"

"Who knows?"

Amy said, "As for Toby Wales, you just pick up all the sons of bitches and put them in a bag and shake it until the real sonofabitch falls out... hopefully an Indian or a black. Is that the process here? That's the way it worked in Philadelphia when Frank Rizzo was mayor."

"No, because Toby is a lot better than that. You covered Philly?"

"As an intern at *Philadelphia* magazine. I worked there during the first semester of my senior year." She twisted her wrist watch up. It was always slipping down under. Her wrist was just bone and I had been noticing her loss of weight. But she wasn't ill; her eyes were clear and she had plenty of energy. "I would have taken their offer of full-time if I hadn't been so angry about how the city ran its campaign against blacks. The magazine didn't get into much controversy, so it would have been constant frustration."

"A wise woman who knows her own heart. I think you have the makings of a star reporter, Kroll. But you're going to have run-ins all your life with the good people who try to make money out of the news."

"And you?"

"I'm compliant as hell. How else can I work where I do?" I wasn't tempted to tell her how close I was to quitting the paper. No sense burdening her with that kind of information. If Everett were to ask her about my plans and she lied and then I quit, she'd be out the door as well.

"Thing is, you don't look like the sharp cookie that you are, Kroll. You're young and pretty, which can work for you, so long as you remain young and pretty."

"Is that sexist talk coming from the free spirited Brew Moore?"

"Let me tell you a story about what is important and what is not. This one is about you, so pay attention.

"There is a Taoist story I found in a novel I was reading the other evening. Seems a Chinese guy, a king of some stature, sees his man who procures horses for him aging and in failing health and can no longer go out and get good horses. The king asks if the older man can recommend someone to take his place. The old horse-acquirer says that there is a talent in finding a fine horse that has shape and stamina and heart. But it takes a genius, someone special with a rare gift, to find a truly superlative horse... one that hardly leaves tracks and is ghostlike, neither here nor there. The essence of horseness, you might say.

"The old Chinese guy advises that his sons can find good horses but do not have the spirit nor genius to find that one truly superlative animal. He adds that he has this small friend, a young man, who is in no way inferior to him. Whereupon the king sends for him and assigns the youngster the mission of finding the almost impossible horse.

"When the boy returns he says he's found one and when asked what kind, he says it's a brown mare. When they bring in the horse it turns out to be a black stallion.

"Well, the king throws a shit fit and wonders at the old Chinese guy, at how he could recommend a boy who didn't know the difference between a brown mare and a black stallion.

"The old Chinese man looks wide-eyed and says, 'Has he

really gotten as far as that?' meaning that the boy is ten thousand times better than the old guy.

"It turns out that the boy keeps his spiritual mechanism in view. He sees the inward qualities and loses sight of the external. He looks for the stuff of life that he must see and he ignores what is unnecessary to observe, such as color and sex.

"The horse turned out to be the best in the kingdom. And Kroll, when I need a fine horse, I'm going to send you out to find it."

"You are such a romantic, Brew Moore," she said, looking off. "How did you survive in the City?"

"I didn't. It ground me into hamburger. What you see here before you now is not a man, it is mere meat. It helped, though, to read and re-read Salinger. So now, this is why I need you to find that one great horse."

"Meaning?"

"Damned if I know. I guess what I'm saying is that I believe in you. For what that's worth."

The pizza finally came and was placed between us and was superb, with all manner of things one would have great difficulty identifying but that crunched nicely and tasted good as long as they were drenched in tomato sauce, garlic and a few kinds of cheese and a companion gulp of Moose Drool. They could have been llama navels and I would still have raved about them, coated as they were.

"Instead of chasing horses tomorrow, I'll be talking to some business people in town," Amy said. "I think I'll do a story on the reaction to three of their own being murdered. Death in a small town taken differently than in the big city. That will be my angle."

"That's a good angle. Wire service may pick it up. But you should be careful. To pre-ordain your angle is to pre-select the truth. Maybe just go out and listen, then come back and ask yourself what you heard."

"Do the wires read our paper?"

"That phone call at home was from an old friend at the AP in New York. If I send it to her, she'll try to get it onto the wire. *Career Building 101* says to write by-lined stories and have the wire snap them up. The next step: *The San Francisco Chronicle*."

"Are you going to work on a piece of the murder story?"

"I'll see Dennis, if he'll talk to me. But until they make an arrest there isn't much for us to do, except what you're doing."

"What about that Arnie Williams guy?" she asked.

"I couldn't bear talking to him, could you?"

She smiled and shook her head no. Jim and Kellog Letwilig were at the bar, eyeing Amy. "Do you know those two over there?" she asked. "They've been undressing me for ten minutes."

"They're okay. That's just the Rock Creek Militia. Harmless drunks at their very best. Pay no mind for they mean no harm. It's just that they don't see many women of quality out here."

"I'm a woman of quality?"

I picked up my beer and toasted her. "If I were half my age, you'd be in big trouble."

She let her smile seep away then and said, "What would you do?"

I went back to the pizza feeling twice my age, smothering my fantasy of what I would do and how she would respond.

"Who do you think did it, Brew?" She took the daintiest bite off the tip end of her combo slice.

"You," I said.

"MMMmmmm," she said, chewing. In a moment, she asked how I'd caught on.

"It's in your eyes."

"My eyes?"

"You have the eyes of a murderer."

"What are murderer's eyes like?" She put her slice down and took a sip of beer.

"Crossed and black — like your heart."

In the best tradition of Western humor, we both kept straight faces.

"No, really. Who do you think did it?"

"Someone like you. I mean, someone normal, not raging, not highly emotional, but with a serious mission. It almost seems like a professional. But not quite. There's some vested interest here that we've got to find. It's in that software project somewhere. If I were to give up my short list right now, I'd have that dandy asshole Mercedes-driving Bob Able at the top. And those two at the bar somewhere in the middle."

"What do you base all this on? I just see three dead people and probably a greedy gunslinger out to rip off an unlucky programmer."

"What's the motive for a professional? There isn't enough money in it, and there are no connections to that world that I can see. No, it's semi-pro and set up to look like a jealous rage."

That was when Kellog Letwilig decided it was time to sidle over and meet the new lady. In the background, as he moved toward us, Jim was raising his voice. "It ain't fer you, piece-a-shit.

Just drink your beer."

Ignoring Jim, Kellog said, "How you doin', Brew Moore?" in his best Clint Eastwood voice. He sat his beer mug down at the end of our table and stood there, ready to stagger as soon as the room would begin a slight spinning. "You get the goods on Peachart yet?"

"Amy, this is Kellog Letwilig — of the Rock Creek Letwiligs. They have a family estate back behind the Red Dog on Lone Mountain." Letwilig nodded at her, his eyes seeming to search for an explanation of why she was here. I expect it was some kind of testosterone-driven situation developing, but what the hell, this was a Montana saloon. I was a little surprised when Amy smiled and looked down. Such a shy gesture for a news hound. Ah well, we are all made up of many parts.

"Seriously," Letwilig continued, "What's been goin' on in town? I been up the Yaak all week clearing property."

"They're working on it," I said.

"They'd better. These guys sit around for months collecting their pay. Then one day something happens, and where are they? Murder is murder, what I always say." He swilled down the last of his beer and dabbed at his beard with a paper napkin.

Amy, fingering her glass and speaking in a quiet, fluttery voice, said that it takes time to collect evidence. "It's got to be bagged and labeled. You can't take a chance on messing up or you can make an arrest but never convict."

"Shit," said Letwilig, looking into his empty can. "Hang the fucker, what I say."

I asked him who he would hang.

"Nearest Indian, what's his name."

"Dennis."

"Dennis O'Brien. Right. I'd shake him until he confessed he done it. Then I'd have a rope party."

Letwilig then decided we'd talked about this subject enough. He jerked his head back and asked Amy if she'd seen the new Red Dog T-shirts back in the corner behind the bar. She hadn't, and he turned and said over his shoulder, "Come on." It was an order and Amy looked at me and shrugged and stood.

"Local color," I said. "Watch the buttons on your blouse." She looked small between the two giant Letwiligs. I decided to put a few bucks into the video poker slots and quit trying to protect every young woman I meet. Bad habit, Brewster. Women love to be protected. Get you into complications, by and by. I shoved a five dollar bill in the slot along with fantasies of winning a cool eight-hundred dollars. The eternal optimist.

# MURDER AT THE RED DOG

After giving up my dollars and sitting back down alone with the brown beer and peanuts, I remembered a gambling joke I'd heard during the day, but when Amy came back and we talked a bit about the Red Dog, I found I'd forgotten the joke and was too embarrassed about my aging memory to say so.

She looked beautiful sitting in the flickering light of a Montana saloon. Or — perhaps it was the work of the Moose Drool.

Surely, indeed, yes indeed — it was the late hour, the grand promise of a dark night and the dark beer. A heavy, good, rich, brown drink in a thick mug at midnight in the outback with a brown-haired woman whose smile made you touch the back of your neck and wish to live forever.

Then it happened. Apparently both Letwiligs found Amy interesting. Jim's voice blew out the lights, almost:

"Fuck you, brother," he said, and he meant it.

It lasted only a few punches because of their size. But Amy and I ducked out and went back to my place and she got out of the car and so did I. I walked with her to her little Volvo, but as she reached the car and as her hand moved out to touch the door, I looked away. I looked away, and she changed her mind. I looked back and saw her hand drop to her side, and she stood as still as the lovely black night around us.

"Do you want to come in, have a late-night Jack Daniel's? Put on Bill Evans.... A little 'All the Things You Are' is good for the soul on a spring night. I'll give you a lesson, tell you what to listen for."

She said nothing. She followed me inside, up the stairs. There was another message on the answering machine and I knew it was Kate again, but the hour was late for a call back. I poured off Jack into the bottoms of two crystal Glenfiddich glasses, put on the CD and opened the French doors to the pre-May air. The air was generous. It told me I had no rights to Amy Kroll who stood close, not touching me, drinking Jack. We felt the pureness of a disappearing winter pressing to us, and the warmth of the cabin behind, and a smiling sweet Jess discreetly out of the way, curled at our feet.

Sometimes, even in winter, love is everywhere, no matter how agile you are or how quickly you are normally able to dodge. I took the glass from her hand and set it and mine on the pub table. Evans's piano was careful, inventive, moody, drifting, quiet, exploring delicate pathways through the tune's changes. I took her in my arms then and she said this wasn't a good idea and

I agreed. "It's a terrible idea," I told her. She lifted her chin and kissed me. "What the hell," I said. "It's April. That's someone's terrible idea, too."

I kissed her then with the April chill to one side and the warmth of the cabin to the other.

The rest of the evening with Amy is really none of your business.

# Chapter Nine

The next morning I discovered it wasn't Kate on the answering box, it was the county prosecuting attorney, Vreeland Peachart. I put on hot water for tea while Amy showered and then called him back and got his secretary. I thought I'd have a fight on my hands getting through to Peachart, but to my surprise, she put me right through.

"We have our assailant," he said. "We're going to haul him in shortly. We're working on the paper work now and the warrant."

"Who is it?" I asked, fully aware that I wasn't going to be told. But that's this job: you have to ask, they have to not answer.

"Now — you know better than that, Brew. But I'll tell you when and where so you can scoop the *Missoulian* and so forth."

Exactly as I predicted. He wasn't running for office now until late summer, but he needed a really good press on this one, which is a crime that would be remembered for several years. Obviously, Peachart wanted to be remembered for the guy who made the arrest in a very tough crime to solve in a very short amount of time, and — ahead of the FBI. One could tell in his voice of the community pressure to get the guy and get a quick conviction.

"Be at my office at four this afternoon. We'll point you in the right direction then."

I started to ask about the examination of evidence but Peachart hung up in the middle of my sentence. I took out the tea bags and went into the bathroom where Amy was drying with a black bath towel. The black against her whiteness made the Cricket edge toward my right ear. He didn't say anything, but he was damned well prepared.

"Here," I said, handing her the mug. "Clear your head a little."

She smiled, leaned toward me and kissed me then ducked back out of any reach I might have been thinking of.

"Should we talk?" I said. "I mean...."

"No," she said, smiling. "Last night was fun, so let's not

get intellectual."

Fine with me, I thought. "Remember our talk about you feeling?"

She clamped the towel around her and tucked in a corner. "Brew, people don't change overnight. I said that last night was fun and it was. It doesn't have to be better or more than that, does it?" She reached for the hair dryer, turned it on then turned it off and looked directly at me. "One thing *did* change overnight: I feel closer to you now. And I like it that way."

The phone rang then and I kissed her on the nose and went off to answer it.

"It's Dennis they're after," the voice on the other end said. No announcement of who it was or anything else. It was a deep, gravely voice from, I judged, the depths of a large-framed body.

"Stenopolis?"

"Of course, dear boy. Oh... sorry, I should have said my name right away, shouldn't I? Oh well, in *ANY* case, Dennis is their suspect and I'm *VERY* frightened for him. You know the pressure to arrest that we've been hearing about. And he is an Indian, which complicates things around here."

"What pressure?" I asked. "It was such an obvious set-up that it'll be laughed out of court."

"Oh, a couple of those fellows who own shops on Main Street, and some others like the idea. I even heard that Bob Able volunteered to be Dennis' defense attorney, that is if he's charged."

"Already? I just talked with Peachart five minutes ago and he wouldn't tell me who he was going after."

"Of course he wouldn't."

"Bob Able hasn't been in court in years. He's a damned tax lawyer, for Christ's sake. That's like being defended by an accountant. Peachart has got to be stopped."

"Which is why I'm talking to you right now. I think you and I have to do something or Dennis is going to be railroaded."

"I'm meeting with him this morning. Maybe he'll have some ideas. Are you sure he *isn't* involved?"

"As sure as anyone can be. What would his motive be, dear boy?"

"I don't know. I don't know which way the investigation is going. But there may be something in that software development project, and there was that eagle feathers stuff... that religious ritual at both scenes. Points so conveniently to an Indian, and Dennis was involved in programming with Gil. You said there was a lot of potential profit."

"I think there was. But remember, he said there were two

projects going on. Dennis and Gil had that separate programming project that was taking up a lot of their time."

"Any ideas about it?" I said.

"Dennis explained it somewhat, and he gave me a small package of disks and a notebook of what he calls documentation. I'm sending it to my brother for safekeeping. I'll tell you more about it when you drop by. Or ask Dennis. It's supposed to be very hush-hush."

"Who's your brother? Where is he?"

"He teaches history at the University in Boulder. His name is Ernest Kassara, and he is truly trustworthy."

"I'm sure he is. We'll talk about that as well. So... Dennis knew a lot of what was going on there, didn't he?"

"But you don't think Dennis is a killer, do you?" she asked in an unusually quiet voice.

"No, but then I've been wrong before. The real question, after you come up with a motive for killing the Owens, is why was Lynette Okla killed? And — is her murder really connected to Gil and Beth's?"

"Just so. Yes, well. But I think we should help Dennis in any way we can."

"What does that mean? Spirit him off somewhere?" I asked.

"If it comes to that, yes," she said.

"No good," I said. "First off, you'd be committing a felony. And they're sure to find him, no matter where he goes. It's always just a matter of time. And then he's *really* convinced them of his guilt. With the technology they have now, anyone who runs just ahead of an arrest will get caught. And if he's an Indian, he probably won't make it alive to the arraignment."

That wasn't true just of Indians here or blacks in the South, or any of those clichés. The law, even in the outback, was still the law. I had probably unreasonable confidence in Peachart. There were some controlled cowboys among them. Nevertheless, a murder suspect on the run, perhaps in the mountains, was pretty damned frightening for both the chasers and the person being chased. The Kootenai Falls community would begin to feel threatened and would probably demand a shoot-on-sight deal. You can take it from there and see the seriousness of running away for Dennis. And yet hanging around and just waiting to get dragged in was hardly a happy alternative. Especially when your attorney, a volunteer way ahead of the game, had virtually no experience in criminal law and hardly any in civil courts and his main interest in life was that red Mercedes.

"Let me talk to him before we do anything at all about this." I said. "Where is he?"

"He was here an hour ago, then went to meet someone. I don't know who. Maybe Bob. Maybe his girlfriend."

"I don't think seeing Greta now is such a good plan. She's got to be in very tough shape."

"He says she's pulled herself together. They spent last night at her place. They were here earlier and we had toast and tea. We called you last evening about ten, but got your answering machine. I hung up because I didn't want to leave a message.... Am I getting paranoid in my old age, Brewster? I was afraid *your* phone was being tapped."

"I don't think they're tapping phones yet. I'd be delighted to think they were. It would mean this isn't so open and shut a case, which I'm afraid it's beginning to look like. You know, Peachart would go down in the political record books in great shape if he got an arrest and conviction in a few weeks. He's definitely looking down the road toward the gubernatorial election. A case like this sewn up neat and tidy practically overnight could be well thought of by Montanans who are getting more nervous every day about crime coming in here."

"Indeed. Well, dear boy, when you see Dennis, make him understand that you and I will do everything we can to help him."

"I will. And if you see him first, give me a call. I'll come right over. I'll be at the paper in a while."

I hung up and looked out of the kitchen window at the bright day. Talking to Stenopolis was like running a two-minute mile, and I needed to catch my breath. Or maybe it was that I'd had just about enough of all this. I came to the mountains for the good life and freedom from complications. Right. It was probably a karma thing and it wouldn't matter where I lit, the same kind of life would engulf me.

Ultimately, what right does a reporter have getting into the middle of a homicide case, I wondered, except to take down the details of the events? Well, again, that's where it is different in a small town in the Outback. I could wade right in, but only to a point. With the Feds around, we all had to watch our butts.

I was thinking of calling Able when Amy came in wearing last night's shirt and jeans. She could wear rags and look as though she stepped out of an ad page in *The New Yorker*.

"That was Stenopolis," I said. "She is very worried that Dennis is going straight to the gallows."

"I don't know him at all," she said, adding that she'd never actually spoken to him but had only seen him working in the back room at the Red Dog.

"Well, I'm going to town and try to find him. I'm probably going to talk to Bob Able. I'm curious about the kind of evidence they've put together and how that's stacking up."

"You don't have to worry about last night," Amy said, smiling. "It's not a worry; it's a good thing. We like each other. That's important."

"Very important," I told her. "How does it rank in importance on a ten point scale?"

"Off the scale," She said.

"In which direction?"

"Guess."

Amy left first, driving away in her old, smoking Volvo. Jessie stood staring at the French doors waiting for me. "Do *you* understand?" I said. "I don't. Women have changed, Jessie. I guess for the better." Jess raced out ahead of me toward the truck looking just once over her left shoulder at the three sheep huddled together against my wood storage building, pretending not to be there.

# Chapter Ten

Lawton Robert "Bob" Able came to Kootenai Falls some ten years ago from the rich east Philadelphia suburb of Merion. He took his law degree from Temple University, and since he was from a staunch Republican family, after a short time with a lobbying organization, he joined Crifton Lutz Solby & Myers. The firm had a large tax practice in Washington, D.C., and L. Robert Able, Esq., became a partner during his second month with them. As far as I could determine, no easy-to-see favors changed hands for that early award. However, the Able family was excessively generous when paying fees for the services of Aaron Solby in the complexities of putting together believable lies for the IRS.

I would have thought a man like Able would have joined a firm such as Kurt Koaler Associates, focused on health care legislation and lobbying arrangements, with close ties to the Republican side of the Congress. For "Bob" Able, as he soon became known, had a high energy, pushy, political manner about him. No one liked him at his first position, as deputy director/federal legislation with First Witness Inc. (FWI), a small lobbying group pushing for a better deal for long-term health-care insurance companies. The laws and regulations prevented insurers from selling high-priced and often redundant coverage to retirees. It was FWI's mission to get the Congress to loosen its stranglehold on the profits of a legitimate American enterprise.

Able thrived in the fierce rush and competitiveness of life inside the Beltway. He was obnoxious and rude to those around him at FWI who had no power. He was anything but a team player, preferring to go it alone, high-pressuring congressional go-fers and aides and even junior representatives and senators who probably saw him as a mover and shaker and were inexperienced enough to think he had some clout in legislative circles. He brushed off anyone he thought unimportant or perhaps less connected or less intelligent than he and ran it alone, garnering as much individual credit as possible. He not only spoke to any and all reporters and Washington watchers, he called *them* with updates and information, always making certain they got his name right and that he appeared somewhere in the story. He was a master at that. I heard it all from a close friend, a source once on the Bob Woodward investigative reporting team at *The Post*. Able's ego, they said, had no bounds, and he would haunt PBS producers and ethical people like Jim Lehrer to get on their shows as an expert. Ultimately, people in Washington are like people anywhere, they bend to pressure. And this guy showed up in hundreds of stories a year and on a dozen television programs such as Larry King, *CBS Evening News with Dan Rather* and those Sunday morning sit-arounds with Tim Russert or Cokey Roberts and Sam Donaldson But one of his closest associates at FWI, a source I called regularly, used to say, in her husky lesbian voice, "You have no idea... what a complete asshole this guy is."

But somewhere out there in ego land something clicked, something didn't go right. He was the object of scorn within his own organization, which isn't unique to Bob Able, obviously. He was among hundreds of similar little men who live for a while on Dupont Circle and try their best to be important. According to reports in *The Post, The Washington Times* and other papers, Able was fired, finally, because all of the high-level lobbyists in First Witness quit and took good jobs with the competition solely because they couldn't stand being around him. A few newsletter releases tried to soften the idea that Washington inner-circle lobbyists walked away because of an asshole upstart bent on furthering his influence regardless of the important bodies he stepped on. One such release made it sound like a lobbyist was leaving to work for a competing firm but "would continue working with us, for which we at First Witness are extremely grateful. In that sense, we are not losing Gail Jordon, as we will be seeing her constantly as we all work toward the same goal of fair legislation for American enterprises."

But the Board of First Witness eventually — if slowly, for such enlightened executives — became aware of Bob Able's destructive arrogance. He wasn't asked to leave; he was offered a job as a consultant to the firm, which reduced his $180,000 a year salary (the CEO position he was angling for would have paid over $400,000 plus enormously attractive benefits, such as car, mortgage payments and the like) to something under $90,000. Humiliating enough to ensure his departure.

He moved over to the tax firm then, but that didn't last long either. In two years, having saved a neat bundle, Able divorced his wife, divorced his children as well, and came up to the good life in Kootenai Falls where, he said, "people are real, there is no miscegenation, races know their places, and the truth means something." That is a quote by Able from *The Wall Street Journal* that I found in a drawer of my desk the first day I worked on the Kootenai Falls paper.

You might say, after all of this, that I didn't like Able very much, and you'd be right. I especially didn't like the fact that a lawyer with his background was going to defend a nice kid in a homicide case that to the prosecution was about as open and shut as they get.

Able met me at the Kootenai Falls Cafe´ at 10:30 a.m., Rita serving us coffee and, where Able couldn't see, curling her lip in a snarl at him, trying to make me break up.

"I couldn't find O'Brien," I said. "Have you seen him?"

"For a few minutes. He doesn't know anything about where he stands."

"What do you mean? Didn't you tell him?"

Able's smile faded. "That would be betraying a confidence." Something was different about him. His hair. His hair was... darker. It looked like a wig, but actually he was coloring it with something. It made the skin of his face seem ghostlike.

"Yeah, a confidence between the county prosecutor and Dennis O'Brien's defense counsel and excluding the accused. Bob, do you think you're the right man for this guy? You're totally inexperienced as a trial lawyer, and your sympathies don't seem in line with your legal obligation to your client." It was clear I shouldn't go on. If he continued defending Dennis and if Dennis was convicted, I would be the star witness for moving to a mistrial. That is, if I kept good notes of this meeting. I couldn't write in front of Able, but I intended to sit right down after this meeting and write down everything that was said.

"The alternative is a court-appointed attorney, and that would be, number one: some twenty-five-year-old with no real world experience and, number two: a law degree about forty-eight hours old. No," he said, touching his sideburns with the fingertips of both hands, "I'm his best hope. Besides, I've been watching Perry Mason reruns." That chilly smile again. with the non-smiling eyes, black hair and bone white face. "In the last analysis, Brew, this is none of your business. It's O'Brien's decision to make, and mine."

Rita refilled our cups without a word and without looking at either of us. Obviously she disapproved of who I was having coffee with.

"That remains to be seen. You're not the best attorney for this job, and I'm hardly sorry if you're offended. Anyway," I continued, "what does the evidence line-up look like? Is there a clear motive?"

"A rape that's not a rape? Looks to me like he had something against Gil Owen and decided the best way to get to him was through his wife. He used a pipe of some kind to penetrate her. Tore her up pretty bad. But she was already dead. Then he stole the software disks to cover it up. Then Dennis made the mistake of not keeping his peyote in his pocket. Indians are so wrapped in their religions that they cannot keep from leaving calling cards, even in murder cases."

"And attempting to kill Greta?"

"We think she was having an affair with Owen. That was a terrible mistake, killing that Okla woman. Brew, we're dealing here with a brainless killer."

What a wonderful attitude for the defense attorney to have. I had to stifle a laugh. Those who knew Gil Owen knew he was incapable of betraying Beth.

"That's a whole lot of horse shit, Counselor. And who is 'we'?"

"Vreeland Peachart, Wales, Russell. We all pretty much see it that way. And as far as I'm concerned, I surely hope you will come around to that view. Number one: it's useless to splinter up and go in a hundred directions and, number two: we'll do better just leaving the investigation to the professionals."

He had this annoying habit of splitting everything into number ones and number twos, whether they went peacefully that way or not. "It sounds more like one of those open-and-shut cases to me. I'll tell you, Counselor, I'd hate to have you for my attorney if I needed one. You're too goddamned cozy with the prosecution for my tastes."

"You might want to look at it another way: I'm close to the prosecution, yes, but that makes me completely informed about their case and how they're lining it up against him. I'm in the best position possible to cut Dennis a plea bargain."

"Plea bargain? Jesus H. Christ, Able, isn't it the most obvious thing in the world that Dennis was set up? And pretty crudely? Also — the prosecution has to show you the evidence anyway, as defense counsel." But there was nothing more to say to him about getting off Dennis' case so I switched gears. "What can you tell me about this Hiram Howell person? Do you know him?"

"Distantly," he said. It was an abrupt answer for Smilin' Bob, and it appeared to me that my question touched something sensitive.

"What do you mean 'distantly'?"

# John Herrmann

"I know *of* him, if that's what you mean. He's a former businessman and a member of the Kootenai Falls inner circle, so naturally none of us new guys who've only been here ten years are asked the time of day by any of them. He's had a wife who gave Sunday lawn parties in the summertime. She died some years ago. What else do you want, and why don't you go ask him?"

"He nearly ran me over the other morning on Seeley and Sixth. An old guy told me Howell acts like he owns the damned street."

"Hiram probably let you live because you're white...."

"Oh, so now it's 'Hiram,' is it?"

"What are you implying? I don't know the man and that's that."

"You don't know him, but you know he's a racist? Well, one other thing, before you pick up the tab: what's this I hear about you traveling with the white supremacist crowd?" Nothing like pushing for the jugular I always say. I watched his eyes, watched for his smile to either brighten or disappear. Neither happened.

"I believe whites are better off with whites and blacks feel more comfortable with their own, if that's what you mean."

"And Indians? You're defending one."

"You're not going to push me into making a statement about being a racist or anything else. I have a widely held opinion about the comfort zone of like-unto-like. That's it. I don't hold with those wild or murderous solutions. I don't believe we're being followed by black helicopters. And by the way, you'll hear a far more militant answer from just about any black man you ever talk to."

"And women? What do you think about women and the feminists?"

"That does it. This meeting is over. Women are whatever they want to be and that's fine with me. I haven't seen you acting like a major backer of that cause. As a matter of fact, you're about as much a macho male chauvinist as those guys you hang out with at the Red Dog." He stood and picked up the check. "And what right do you have questioning me about my politics? What in hell does that have to do with me defending a murderer?"

"Plenty. It'd be nice to know that Dennis' counsel has no particular ax to grind about race purity, since his girlfriend is, as you say, white. And by the way, you're not defending a murderer, you're defending someone *accused* of murder. There's a difference, and I'm sure if Dennis O'Brien were here he would have liked you to have seen that difference."

"Manner of speaking, Brew. So — anyway — you know

where the investigation is going and you know as much as I do. Now just keep the proper distance from both me and my client and I won't have to do anything about asking the County Attorney to *make* you keep your distance."

He walked up to the counter, paid and left without looking back at me. I watched through the front window as he swung open the Mercedes door, got in and sped off toward the Court House.

# Chapter Eleven

After spending a few minutes writing up my meeting with Able, I went to the phone trying to find someone who had seen or heard from Dennis. Apparently he was still nowhere to be found. A while later I ran into Russell Pace in the Post Office. I stopped him, asking exactly what got the FBI involved in a local homicide.

"Mr. Moore, as I said before, we don't discuss ongoing investigations."

"Yeah, I know," I said. "But I'll bet your PR guys in Salt Lake will give me a proper answer on this one because it really looks like you're going beyond your jurisdiction."

"If you were just a resident here, I could talk to you a little. But you're the press. Whatever I say, no matter what or where, is for publication. My hands are tied." He straightened up and showed me his wrists clamped together.

"And I also thought you guys always worked with partners."

"The new FBI is very different from the Bureau of your memory, Mr. Moore. You should take a refresher course. It's really quite interesting. And we cooperate with local law enforcement far more than in previous years."

"Listen," I said, "what if I absolutely promised off-the-record?"

"Sorry." He left the building then, grim-faced, walking quickly across Main Street, passing the library that was next to the court house that also housed the sheriff's office... all on the same block.

The FBI doesn't run unless something is seriously wrong.

Back at the office, Amy was writing furiously and did not look up as I brought Jessie in and she slid under my desk. There was a note on my desk to call a toll free number and ask for room 121.

The voice that answered told me everything in an instant.

"Kramer's River Inn," said the woman.

"Room 121, please."

In a moment, a muffled male voice answered with a tentative "Hello?"

"Dennis?"

"Brew?"

"What are you doing in Idaho?"

"How'd you know it was me? I just left a number."

"Just a wild guess, kid, but the receptionist gives the location of the motel. I put two and two together and it spelled *panic attack*."

"They were coming to get me and charge me with those shootings, Brew. So I took my lawyer's advice and took off. Give 'em time to catch the real killers so they don't just stop lookin' with me in jail is what he told me."

I couldn't agree with him more. Dennis had done exactly what I would have. But I couldn't tell him that. I looked over and saw Tom and Amy looking at me, trying to read the conversation.

"Well, son, you're not exactly in the wilderness now, are you? I mean, how hard would it be to find you?"

"I'm not staying here, but I don't want to be out of contact. I need to know what's going on."

"What about Able? Can you call him? If you call me, eventually someone will figure it out."

"Bob Able told me the dangers of running. He also told me the dangers of staying. He said I should not keep him in the dark about anything."

"But be careful trusting anybody, Dennis. You should think about getting a public defender and dump Able."

"That means coming back. That's not an option right now, Brew."

"So — where are you headed?"

"I'm not sayin' because I don't want to put you under that burden. Somebody there knows, though, and..."

"Your lawyer?"

"I'm not sayin' who. They'll go to jail if the police find out."

"Not your lawyer. He's covered by the attorney-client privilege. But how do I figure into this?"

"I know you're on the Internet with e-mail. You can leave me messages and I can check it wherever I am without a trace. All I need is a phone line." He gave me his America On-Line address then. "You and I can communicate and no one can find out where I'm receiving the messages."

"When did you find out they were going to charge you?"

"They were diggin' in my yard. I knew with the other

stuff, like the feathers, that somebody was settin' up Chief Wahoo."

"Is it Greta who knows?"

"I won't say, Brew. I told you that."

"Well, at least tell me if you're going to stay close or go to Alaska or something."

But the line went dead and I heard the sound of my own voice dead-ended in that flat, unconnected, helpless manner of a one-sided telephone conversation. Goddamn but I hate being hung up on.

To clear one thing up right here — I never heard from Dennis on the Net or any other way.

"O'Brien?" Everett asked.

"The one and only," I said. "Our favorite assailant. He figured it out and took off running."

"They'll find him quick enough," he said.

Amy frowned: "Why'd he call *you*?"

"I think because Stenopolis confirmed that he could trust me. Dennis absolutely trusts her and Leo. He and I go back a long way, but you never know. People change. And the Stenopolis' have been like family to him."

"You got any idea where he's headed?" Everett asked.

"No, and if I did I wouldn't tell you or anyone else. Not that I don't trust you. That's not the point."

"I understand," Amy said.

"Well I don't," said Everett, slamming his flat hand on his desk and sending papers and pens flying onto the floor. Jessie's head popped up as well. "You either work for this paper or you don't. And this time I mean it. If you have any special information about these murders and the investigation, then you will either take it to the investigators or you'll clean out your desk."

Roxy was standing in the doorway of her office watching the goings on, one hand on her hip. I stood up then and motioned for Jess to come out from under my desk. "There's nothing in the desk I need, Tom. All the background stuff for the cougar piece is in the computer. Amy or you can put it together from that."

"Now Brew," Roxy said, "Tom is just worried that...."

"I know. I don't want him to have to worry." Amy was sitting hunched over her keyboard, not moving, not breathing. "No hard feelings, Tom. This just isn't working for either of us."

He turned away then, nodding. In a way, we got along and had mutual respect and common interests in what regional stories were good for a community paper. But that was not enough. It was time for me to walk.

Jessie ran out ahead of me. "I'll see you all at the Red Dog tonight or tomorrow, Tom, Roxy," I said. "Forward my calls, please." I left the office, got Jessie into the truck and got in and sat for a moment feeling free. I never should have taken the job in the first place, which is exactly what Kate Wells told me when I left New York.

Suddenly, Amy was at my side window. "I know. Don't tell me," I said. "I'm an impulsive...."

"No. There's a press conference about to start in the Court House."

"Get in," I said.

# Chapter Twelve

It was a tiny room for a conference of any kind, but there were just a few reporters. There was one from Missoula, others from Bozeman, Helena, Billings, an AP guy from Salt Lake, the Spokane paper, a freelancer, Amy, me and Jessie who dutifully curled up next to my chair.

Vreeland Peachart welcomed us and introduced the investigators Wales and Pace.

"Thank you for coming, ladies and gentlemen," Peachart began. "I just wanted to clear up a few things this afternoon about the status of the investigation into the three homicides, which is the third day of the investigation. We had hoped to arrest a suspect by now. As it turns out, our suspect has disappeared. I'll have more on that in a minute."

A few shouts from the press ruffled Peachart for a moment, but he continued, ignoring the questions.

"FBI Agent Russell Pace and I and our associates thoroughly searched both crime scenes and found evidence there as well as at the alleged assailant's home to definitely connect one Dennis O'Brien to the three homicides."

Since none of the reporters except Amy and me had ever heard of Dennis, there was no murmuring, merely note-taking. I also sensed disappointment in Peachart that the occasion had not registered as important enough to send over a TV news crew. He had gotten himself prepared, just in case, wearing a navy blue suit, light blue dress shirt and a red power tie. It was obviously his wedding and funeral suit, high-style Italian, circa early 1980s — narrow lapels, single-breasted, butt flap.

"To recap what many of you already know, there have been a total of three homicides, each victim shot once in the head, and one victim appeared to have been raped. That victim was ElizaBeth Grace Owen, thirty-six. We were fortunate in getting immediate action by our Missoula lab — and the report stressed 'appearance of rape,' as there was no evidence of, um, normal penetration. No body fluids or pubic hairs found on the victim.

# MURDER AT THE RED DOG

"Her husband, Gilbert Edward Owen, was thirty-six as well. Each of these two victims died instantaneously. The third victim, Lynette Okla Williams, age forty-four, apparently remained alive for quite some time. However, the County Coroner believes she was unconscious during that time.

"We found pieces of peyote at the scene of the two Owen murders in the back of the Red Dog Saloon, which appears to be from either Hopi or a Blackfeet Indian religious ritual. Russell Pace ran an FBI check on the peyote and we can report definitely that it is Hopi. Our suspect is also Hopi. Neither the Red Dog rear area nor Greta Hahn's residence show any signs of forced entry. The perpetrator had access to both scenes with either keys or else he was admitted because he was known to the victims.

"In addition, early this morning we found the murder weapon — a .357 magnum caliber Smith and Wesson revolver — buried in the suspect's backyard. Ballistics found a match with the bullets from both scenes, and our crime lab expert here," pointing to Toby Wales, with chuckles all around the room, "reports the weapon had been wiped clean of prints. However, the location of the weapon is circumstantial evidence, as are the other aspects. But Agent Pace here, after exhaustive interrogation of dozens of townspeople, found a citizen who can place Dennis at the Red Dog late on the afternoon of those two murders. In addition, we have the suspect's fingerprints on the disks containing the ad blocking software we told you about earlier."

Which of course wouldn't hold up in any court, as Dennis was a co-developer. He would have been cut in on the profits.

I raised my hand and was ignored.

"What do you want to know?" Amy asked.

"I want him to identify the witness who placed Dennis at the Red Dog."

Peachart continued, saying that his office would not reveal the name or names of any witnesses that his office would call during the trial, saying that is was for their own protection.

"Protection from a missing suspect?" I shouted.

"We're not taking chances," he said. "We think he might be up Kootenai Falls Creek in the Cabinet Wilderness. But with this weather coming in, he won't stay there long."

"Do you have search parties going in after him?"

"Not as such. We've positioned deputies at trail heads. But the depth of the snow up there is more our friend than his, if we keep out of it.

"I'd like to add that the FBI is involved in this case..."

At last! I was wondering if they would have to play straight with all of the press around.

"... because of the ad blocking software and interstate commerce law."

So, they were going that far to get the federales involved. Questions came from the press concerning the nature of the infraction, and the whole story of the software development project came out. Peachart let Pace explain that it is illegal to subvert purchased advertising air time, even by electronic means. "At best," he explained, "Gilbert Owen and Dennis O'Brien should have requested that the U.S. Congress consider the law and alter it to accommodate their goals. The addition of their software, as I understand it, blocks whatever is generated between electronic impulses. It's similar to those small flashes one sees that alerts film projectionists that it's time to change reels. Between those electronic impulses we get those strings of commercials. What the Owen-O'Brien software accomplishes is an audio and video blackout between those impulses."

Someone asked: "Are you also charging the financial backers?"

"At present, we don't know who they are. We'll take that up later when and if it's appropriate."

"So," Amy asked, "what's the motive for the killings?"

"Good question," I said. "Nail them now or they'll slip out of it later."

"Greed, Miss Kroll."

I was surprised that Pace knew her by name.

"There was a remarkable first-buy payoff of over three-million dollars offered by one of the small satellite dish manufacturers. We presume that O'Brien didn't want to share it. Also, he was, in every sense of the word, a junior partner. Gilbert Owen was the programmer; Dennis O'Brien merely carried out his instructions. We theorize that O'Brien well understood that he could easily come away with nothing more than salary for assisting in the development."

"Can you charge the TV satellite company?" someone asked.

"One thing at a time. We have the originators here, and that was my assignment — to find out what the software was, what it could do, who developed it and who, in the end, would profit from it. Anything more than that is up to the Bureau."

Vreeland Peachart took over the mike again when the question of the motive for the murder of Lynette Okla was raised.

"She was mistaken for Greta Hahn by the accused. It was dark and apparently the assailant didn't know the victim was staying at Miss Hahn's home on the night of the murder. He merely went in and shot a woman who was the same height, build, basic coloring of his girlfriend."

"Do you have any information or speculation as to why he would want to kill his girlfriend?"

"I didn't want to get into this now," Peachart said, "but I'd better clear it up. We have information from sources who will testify that Gil Owen and Greta Hahn had been more than friends. So we're looking at jealousy as the motive for that killing as perhaps the other two. That it was the wrong woman makes no difference. We are charging willful homicide and consider it a triple murder."

I looked at Amy. "That's a lot of killing for a guy who never committed a single crime in his whole life. You don't buy it, do you?"

"When you're logical like this..."

"Yes?"

"... and when you treat me like an equal..."

"Yes?"

"And when you really, really want to know what I think..."

"Yes?"

"You make me so damned horny that I think I'll have to go home and change my underpants."

"Amy" I said, whispering in her ear, "you like sex, don't you?"

She blushed and looked down.

The young man sitting near us pretended not to hear. He was looking down at his reporter's notebook.

I ran into Attorney Able on the way out of the building. "I guess I'll attend to some business," he said. "At least until they round up my client and haul him in for an arraignment. Here," he said, handing me his card. "My cellular phone number is on that. Call me when they find Dennis. Vreeland and my assistant are also going to call. But just in case, you phone, too."

"Where will you be?"

"I've got tax returns for several businesses and it's pretty spread out. One in Kalispell and three in Spokane. I ought to at least get Kalispell finished and off to the IRS before I have to come back for this. I keep the cell phone with me all the time, so I'll be in touch."

At Stenopolis' house later I asked about going back through the store.

"It's pretty well locked up," she said. "We're not going to even *think* about doing anything with the building or the stock until this is all over."

"I'm thinking there may be something in there or around the place that would possibly help Dennis."

"Like what?"

"I have no idea, just an inclination not to give up." I told her about my final run-in with Tom Everett and said I had all the time I needed now to help Dennis, if he was innocent.

"Oh, he's innocent all right. But proving it is another matter."

"It's up to Peachart to prove his guilt, not the other way around."

"Life ought to be like that. But you know and I know how it really works."

"One good thing, even if the prosecutor is a jerk, Toby Wales is a decent human being and a fine, professional detective. Kootenai Falls is damned fortunate to have a guy like him and a bunch of tough and smart guys in the sheriff's department.

"By the way, I'll want to see those disks you sent to your brother. Does anyone else know where they are?"

"Not even of their existence. Leo doesn't even know. Just you and I."

"And Able?"

"I don't trust him, Brewster. I've told him nothing."

"Tell me the truth — do you know where Dennis is headed? He told me that he confided in one person here, and it wasn't me."

"He told me not to acknowledge anything or any contact with him. But yes, he told me. But I won't tell you or anyone else."

"Does Able know that you know?"

"I think he may, but I haven't said anything."

"Well, we'll see what a dedicated defense counsel he is, won't we?

# Chapter Thirteen

With Able out of town and the townspeople all but forming a posse, Stenopolis had to be very careful about who she spoke to about any of this. But I got the key from her to the back room of the Red Dog and Jessie and I drove out Rock Creek.

Nothing much was out of the ordinary inside. The stock had been examined but was still pretty much on shelves and orderly. The back storage room was nearly empty, as most of the disks, tapes and records had been boxed and carted off by sheriff's deputies. I also noticed that the security system had been turned off. A camera attached to a television and VCR near the back entrance were also turned off. Nothing electric or electronic was on except a large wall clock above an IBM computer. It was dark inside and even Jessie walked around carefully, unable to clearly see where she was going. I didn't want to touch any wall switches because there might still have been the need to search for fingerprints. The only other light was a tiny red glowing from the stack of televisions and VCRs near the doorway designed to make the occasional retail customers stop and look at themselves and then the merchandise.

There was a small motorized connection to the camera and TV that caused it to move and follow anyone in view around the room. The camera moved but the VCR and TV were not on. Tiny red dots above the cameras at the corners in the ceiling were also lit. I'd seen the police searching the control unit for a tape, but there was none. Either Gil hadn't loaded it, or the killer had wisely made off with the tape.

Gil's security system hadn't done him or Beth much good as it was devised to discourage theft, not murder.

I closed my eyes and tried to take Gil backward in time from the moment of the shot. He'd come through the doorway into the store to find his wife — dead already, or a gun to her head? But where had Gil come from? Where was his car parked? I hadn't seen it in the lot to the east side of the building. Had he run in after hearing Beth's screams? And had she actually screamed, or was she told to be silent? Silence could mean she knew her killer. And was there a single killer or two, or maybe three? I also had to drive from my thoughts the fact that, of course, the killer could have been Dennis after all. I had to keep reminding myself that we just didn't know, and if you don't know something you cannot proceed as though you have figured part of it out.

One thing I did know: while the murders were violent, there was little need for force. A gun is plenty of leverage and you don't need strong-arm tactics. Also, there was the almost certainty that the rape was faked. It was done after Beth died as a kind of mis-direction. Obviously, the reason for the homicides was not to accomplish a rape.

Outside in back of the Red Dog, it's red neon lights glowing up into a black night, Jessie nosed through the snow and I stood there in the doorway watching her and trying to figure out why anyone would think a set-up like this would work to incriminate Dennis. It was too obvious and far too neat to be believable. Peyote pieces at the scene and a buried gun were too easy. Maybe the prosecution would go the route of presenting the evidence as though Dennis had set himself up in an obvious way to throw off suspicion. But then what physical evidence was there to justify bringing him to trial?

I went back inside and sat on a stool near the stack of televisions. The coils of black wire had seen it all happen. Snakes of cable and brass wire were the only witnesses. The black TV screens and green computer monitors all had reflected the shootings. If one could merely scrape the outer layers of glass one might set a wire to the mound of glass to reconstruct images of the past. They *were* all there — images and drama embedded in glass. The dead-eyed cameras as well. The air and the patterns of dust had all been displaced in exact proportion to the features and gestures of both killer and victim. At a future time, crime scene reconstruction would include all of these things. But not now. Now we might as well exist in caves for all the reading we can do of our surroundings and the events that take place in them.

I have heard that a sharp object like a needle connected to a speaker can be threaded into the grooves of an ancient piece of pottery and by spinning the pot, one can hear the actual sound of the potter's wheel from 15,000 years ago. It has been described as a rumbling with occasional thumps because the wheels were primitive and unbalanced.

It is not beyond human capability to bring back the image of a crime from shavings of a television screen. It is only so now.

# Chapter Fourteen

When Dennis had been missing for an entire week, the Letwiligs, Hiram "the nut" Howell, and some of the frequenters of the local bad-ass bars had all but formed a posse. If the weather had been warmer, they all would have been in the mountains south of Kootenai Falls with their hunting rifles. It was the middle of the first week of May as it was, and with that came a serious and dangerous thaw with avalanches, flooding and mud slides. Part of the west side of town was in serious trouble, with two small doublewides having slid into the river's edge. But for now, it was mostly quiet, frozen in the perennial shady areas, and the mountains impenetrable. Most of the people of Kootenai Falls had returned to their normal routines, which in May is the tail end of a winter's sleep.

I'd heard that Hiram Howell had creamed yet another unwary motorist who had wandered, innocent, uninformed and under-insured, onto Seeley Street; Russell Pace had returned to the FBI Field Office in Salt Lake City, his portion of the investigation apparently in the bag; Vreeland Peachart had successfully convinced the Kootenai Falls business inner circle that justice would win out. The way one of the loggers put it: "As for getting this killer — *it will be did*!"

The days slipped by and an easier feeling toward Tom Everett had replaced my initial anger and disappointment in having come three-thousand miles for a position that I held for so short a time. And Kate Wells had been out of town on assignment for over a week, so that I had not even had my usually generous share of nagging from her about going out and getting a real career position.

And Amy? Sweet Amy.... I hardly saw her at all. Tom had handed her the load of stories I would have done along with her own. Until someone came to town with even fair credentials, she'd be doing two writing jobs. That's the way Tom worked: he didn't seek reporters and replacements because he wanted it to be a buyer's market. His theory was that if someone came in, hat in hand, asking for work, they would be more likely to be grateful and, so, work all the harder for low pay.

Amid my musings as to what to do next and doing a little training of Jessie, I decided that I was the only thing Dennis O'Brien had going for him, and if I didn't keep working on his behalf, pretty soon he wouldn't have a behalf. So I called Greta Hahn, who agreed to talk to me as long as I had no connection with the newspaper and as long as I didn't tell Dennis that she was going to be a witness for the State

"You are? What on earth did you witness?" I said. "You were out of town down at the Swan when the murders took place."

"Dennis told me over and over about how he was being cut out of the financial part of the software project," she said. "Besides, I'm just one witness. That's what I know and I have to tell it. I'd be subpoenaed anyway, they said."

"Okay. You have to testify. But you don't have to offer anything. Remember that. And please try to remember that Dennis is innocent... at least until they prove he did it."

She narrowed her eyes. "That's easy for you. No one tried to kill you. There is still someone out there who believes he has reason to see me dead, and it could be Dennis." She turned her head to the side. "You have no idea what this is like. Every noise, every car that goes by and slows.... I have to think about whether to switch on a light or to risk going to Safeway for milk and eggs or just go hungry and play it safe. Is playing it safe really staying here where the killer knows exactly how to get to me?"

She must have been a pretty little girl, but the decades had not been kind to her. Heavy drinking and smoking had brought deep worry creases to her forehead and vertical wrinkles to her upper lip. The skin of her throat sagged and thick veins stood out on the backs of her hands where liver spots had already formed. Even just barely in her forties, she already had that hard Montana face. Someone once wrote that the face of Montana is one not for sociability but merely a face to face the weather. I would not describe faces I have seen in that way, but it has the ring of truth when applied to Greta Hahn.

She was surely not someone you would think of as the target of a jealous lover.

I knew next to nothing about her, other than having seen her a few times with Dennis at these small events that occur at Christmas in small American towns. Her house told me very little about her except that she spent hardly any time in it. There was an office of sorts in the dining room, a few small pretend Persian carpets in the living room and hallway; dishes in the kitchen sink had piled up with food crusted on them. "Disorder and early sorrow" seemed to characterize Greta Hahn, and the sad truth was that I could see little life in her, as if she could simply lie down on the floor at my feet, breathe a final time, and relax into that last good sleep. She was the prototypical small-town middle-aged, unmarried, disappointed woman you have read about in stories by Sherwood Anderson and John Steinbeck. I thought then — with her standing before me teary-eyed and fearful — that Dennis must have taken pity on her. That was the only explanation I found for a handsome, smart young fellow spending his nights, his youth and his semen on her.

Do I sound cruel? Heartless? Well, I have little patience with good people who give up and let life become as interesting as an empty shopping cart. In the beginning, Greta must have had dreams. In nursing school, she must have thought at least once about helping diminish suffering in the world. So if I am being hard on her — and I may be — I am also being hard on myself. Little by little — *poco a poco* — I have sunk from idealism, from liberalism, from activism, from many many many *isms*, to watching the shadows move as the sun rises, watching Jessie walk slowly and forcefully behind her sheep through the thinning snow from one field to the next. It was happening in me and of course I saw it in Greta and was critical of what I saw.

"All right," she said finally. "I'll tell you. But you cannot tell anyone else. Do you understand?"

I was confused. I hadn't counted on her telling me anything much. I had simply wanted to get a feeling for Dennis' private existence. Something of the reality of his life might help me help Bob Able defend him.

"Dennis and Gil were working on a program to withhold advertising on TV. It was finished and sold. But there were competing buyers who wanted to buy it and kill it by owning it, and some of them were not very well mannered, according to Dennis."

That didn't figure with what Stenopolis had been saying about two software projects, but it was probable that the other project was so hush-hush that they didn't let Greta in on it. Also, the second program didn't appear to have the financial implications of blocking out TV advertising.

"The networks must have been fuming over this."

"Yes," she said. "Dennis said there had been an extraordinary offer to kill the project by someone who said he was representing all three networks. But you know, Dennis was funny about talking much. You know that it's not manly for a Hopi to be verbal."

We talked of her own security and I suggested we could arrange a safe haven in Missoula where I have friends. Although nervous about staying in Kootenai Falls, she said she was more nervous about leaving. She said she'd feel more vulnerable.

# Chapter Fifteen

When we talked about hiding her in Missoula again, I wondered if Leo could drive her, I said she could stay with a friend of mine from the old days. I told Greta that I would have Amy contact her when, and if, it was safe and appropriate for her to return to Kootenai Falls. But she was adamant about not wanting to move that far, that she was more afraid of being on the road. She said Alesandra had invited her to stay with her and Leo's. "Besides," she said, "I have friends here who would take care of me. And I'm a nurse, I have a few of the old people I have to take care of."

That was fine with me, except that she wouldn't be difficult to find if someone really tried. But it was her call.

I didn't recognize the voice of the bargirl who answered the phone at the Red Dog. It turned out to be a neighbor of mine who has made me some of the finest pizzas humans of this earth have ever tasted. I just walk into the place and see her and the first thing that pops into my head is — cholesterol.

I asked her to call Jim Letwilig to the phone. While I waited, I watched outside to see if Jessie was at the truck's window. She'd been packed in there for hours and it was going to be time to give her a bladder break.

When Jim answered I told him I needed to talk to him right away.

"Yeah?" He sounded grumpier than usual, as though I'd taken him away from his favorite slot machine while he was on a rare winning streak.

"First of all, I quit the paper, so this isn't about that."

"You quit your job? Jobs around here are pretty goddamned hard to find."

"I saved a little money so it's not a tragedy. But listen, I want to talk about something and I can't talk about it on the phone or at the Red Dog."

"So, where *can* you talk?"

"Meet me in fifteen minutes at Fiedler Park?"

He grunted something in the receiver and hung up. I assumed it was a "yes."

Jessie sniffed around for five minutes to find an appropriate spot for a truly major whiz and then spun around and looked at me with the intensity of a miler at the starting blocks. "Sorry, old girl, no walk for a while." Her ears dropped and she turned her attention to a section of snow where tufts of grass grew, protected by young larch and ponderosas. There were round impressions in the snow and grass as though a few deer had spent the morning snooze time there. She rooted around and came up with a dopple of snow on the end of her black nose.

Finally, Jim's blue Nissan pickup showed up. It was still moving as he pushed the door open and started working on extricating his huge frame from the little truck.

"What's so important I can't drink beer with the talk, Mr. Brew Moore?" He was wearing a dirty baseball cap with the NAPA Auto Parts logo on it. The cap was too small for his head of thick hair and stood on top like something a kid would wear to a birthday party. His grimy once-white T-shirt had half a day's work cutting fire wood on it, along with some of his breakfast.

"Do you still have contact with guys in the Montana Militia?"

"Oh shit," he said, pulling off the cap and turning around. Jessie's head came up out of the grass, snow on her black nose, and she studied Jim for a moment. She didn't like quick movements around me by people who carried firearms in the trucks.

"I don't mean to pin you down to anything, I just want to know if you know anyone I can talk to about that Trooper list thing, and maybe about e-mail between groups."

He began unbuttoning his Levi's to take a leak. Standing with both hands on his hips, he spoke over his shoulder: "I could maybe answer your questions. But I ain't putting you on to none of them guys." He finished, buttoned up with one hand and said, "It's not a tea party. These guys are serious about what they do."

"Which is why I want to talk to them and find out about their Internet links. I'm thinking one of the more off-the-wall guys could be involved here."

"You bleeding hearts just never like it when one of your minorities pulls something like this. You gotta look around for somebody else to blame. Let me tell you, if the Indian did it, the liberals ain't gonna get him off. It might work like that back East, but you're in Montana now, and we don't stand still for no ACLU crap. Up here we still believe in the Constitution."

"And you don't think the ACLU believes in the Constitution?"

"Yeah... the *communist* constitution."

"Let me ask you... do you know who killed Gil and Beth?"

"I don't know nothin' about who killed nobody."

"Did you do it?"

He looked at me with narrowed eyes and slammed his cap back onto the top of his hair, then broke on in a broad grin. "You're such an asshole, I can't help but like you."

"Same to you, too, Letwilig. I think Greta Hahn is in danger. And I think whoever killed those three people would like to see Dennis dead rather than have him go to court."

"All this killing isn't like the guys I know." He was leveling now. His voice was lower and calmer and you could see he was trying to think through his thoughts. "Ain't one of 'em would kill people like the Owens, or some nurse. But people better watch their ass if they're with the federal government. Randy Weaver never would a drawd no gun on nobody if the ATF wouldn't a pushed."

"I know all the stories, Jim. You don't have to recite the litany. But I think you can help me out here, and help the community, let alone a couple of innocent people like Dennis and Greta."

"How's that?"

"Let me see your Internet stuff on the militias. Walk me through the stuff, or print it out. Point me in a direction. Otherwise, you know Able and Peachart will get away with railroading Dennis O'Brien and it won't be long before Greta Hahn is no longer whinnying with us."

In true Montana-macho form, Jim turned and silently worked his frame back into his little Nissan truck. I'm supposed to know what he's thinking. He started the engine, gave me the finger and said, "You bring the beer."

# Chapter Sixteen

You can make all Letwiligs except Jim happy with a six-pack of Keystone. Jim, of course, preferred Johnny Walker Red... when he could afford it. The rest of the pack could become ecstatic over a half-case of Coors. "Pussy beer," they call it. "Coors Light is Coors with a different label's all. It's all just water," they always say, drinking the pussy beer down in two gulps and smashing the aluminum can on the floor with their boot. It was a show of toughness, but a toughness unlike what a man was really like a hundred years ago on this same land. Like running and other contemporary exercise is a replacement for hard farm work, smashing aluminum cans replaces a hard life of digging post holes for fencing on nothing but beans, bread and water, with a quart of whiskey on Saturday night and a glimpse of a pretty girl in a white dress in the distance five or six times a year. Jim Letwilig — close to seven feet tall — wouldn't last one summer afternoon working on a ranch in 1897. But it was fun pretending.

We booted the MacIntosh and Jim connected to the server and got into his e-mail. There were 41 messages, most from something called Starmen. He said it was better than Trooper for skinheads and folks who dislike Jews, blacks, reds, greens, yellows.... There were jokes about liberals, and many unflattering ones about women. "If you spread a gals legs what kind of punctuation do you get? Answer: it looks like an exclamation point!"

The level of anger is astonishing: ... *so liberal judges and lawyers have failed with their unconstitutional law to force school integration and bussing in crushing the white race. Now these liberal pigs, such as writers like the Jews Norman Mailer, Jacob Liebling, and Rod Stein say the solution is forcible integration of neighborhoods. HUD subsidizes city blacks who move into white suburbs. BUT LITTLE DO THESE PIGS KNOW THAT THESE TACTICS JUST STRENGTHEN OUR CAUSE?...*
and —

*... When the President of the United States signs a treaty with a foreign power and it is ratified that it becomes the supreme law of the land, superseding all federal and state laws including*

*the Constitution. How long will it take for the kikes and their nigger lackeys have total control of the money and therefore the strength of our white heritage? We must have an action plan to keep Abe and Willy Brown where they belong which is back in the hot sands of Israel which they stole from the A-rabs anyway, and the blacks back in the jungles with the rest of the jigaboos...*

I left Jim's place with a press kit from The National White Party. "Be careful with that," he said. "It's a model." And it was that. Very slick, very professional, and obviously done by a major ad agency. I drove down the road a mile to the Red Dog and sat outside in the car and thumbed through the newsletters that were included in the kit. If Gil Owen was dancing around with this type of company, it's not hard to wonder what he was working on besides blocking advertising.

I jumped into the Red Dog and grabbed a six-pack of Coors, snapped a can open and got back on the road to the singing of an excited border collie just bounding from window to window and shoving her smiling bandit-masked face out into the wind, tongue flying like a pink rope.

The next stop would be the newspaper and a talk with Tom. Greta needed protection. One way was to get her a new location for a while, but she wanted to stay close by. As I said, that was her call. But another way to protect her would be to reveal the nature of the software project to the world through the paper. If everyone knew that computer software could eliminate TV advertising, there would be no more secret for Greta to keep. But would Tom cooperate?

No, of course not. Tom was not in a cooperative mood and would not use his paper to broadcast a computer project like that thereby pissing off the world of advertising.

"Think of this newspaper as a nice, quiet mama and papa retirement business not unlike those little corner grocery stores we knew as children," he said.

The phone rang then and Tom picked it up. I sauntered over to where Amy was pounding on her keyboard. "Will you have a little time for dinner tonight?" I asked.

She nodded but said nothing. I said I'd call about the time but was interrupted by Tom.

"It's over," he said quietly.

Amy stopped working and looked up. Roxy came out of her office.

"They found Dennis," Tom said. "Dead."

# Chapter Seventeen

I spread out angel hair pasta on Amy's and my plates and handed over the pot of sauce for her to do it herself. I poured off yet another glass of Mouton Cadet Bordeaux (1992, if you must know) and sat with her at my pub table.

"Have you asked yourself why he went all the way down to Taos?" I said, siphoning off the overfill of my glass. The strong red wine was exactly right for the heaviness of this evening. Yet another death, yet another crime, and all Peachart and Everett and the rest of them could say was "At last it's over." Well, it wasn't *over*. As far as I was concerned, we were exactly where we were two weeks before — at square one. With one or more murderers dancing free as wild turkeys in the woods.

"When in trouble, head for home," she said, handing me the sauce pot. It was a tomato sauce with generous amounts of garlic and onions, basil, a whisper of cayenne, parsley, sunk into a few tablespoonfuls of extra virgin olive oil, then seasoned with a half-cup of Merlot.

"Home was Arizona, I thought. Aren't Hopis from Arizona?"

"New Mexico is close enough," she said. "Or maybe he was on his way. They think he knew the owner of the Inn pretty well. We heard that from the Taos cops."

"They got Dennis' killer pretty fast."

"Too fast," she said. "Mmmm, this sauce is fantastic."

"Don't compliment with your mouth full. What's the guy's name they're holding?"

"Gordon something. Allard, I think. Called a guy I know in Taos who said he was the town crazy. They said he was a schizophrenic at first, then that he is a manic depressive who won't take his Lithium. Acts out all sorts of weird stuff all the time, threatens people. Really out of control at times, then a very quiet mannerly person at other times."

The Mouton Cadet was heavy and I sipped at it and thought a moment. Then I told her that if Peachart was closing the book on this, I'd be going down to Taos. "You don't call off the dogs when your suspect gets killed. That's too easy. And it's too convenient that the Taos town nut was the instrument to put the lid on."

"MMMmmmm," she said, agreeing with her mouth full. There was love in her dark eyes for my spaghetti sauce, if not for me. "Do you want company?"

A delightful idea but hardly practical. She had her work here, and I had my emotional cement wall to maintain. Traveling down the highways with Amy could only lead to an erosion of my will to remain loveless and reclusive.

"Not this time," I said. Thinking it was one thing; saying it was another. It didn't feel good telling her I didn't want her to come along.

"You could pleasure me at your will," she said, holding her fork out as though it were bait.

"Where is that '90s woman now? But for one thing, I'm not going to make this a quick trip. I won't fly."

"You're going to drive so you don't have to leave that dog."

"I'd love nothing better than to get on the road." I didn't want to tell her about Stenopolis' brother in Boulder, Colorado, with those disk copies, and that the quickest way to Taos by car from Kootenai Falls was east to Billings then south on I-25 right past Boulder.

"That's at least a two days. It's the dog, Moore, isn't it? Come on, admit it. You really are married to that goddamned dog."

"Doesn't matter. It's a great drive. But will you do something for me?"

She cocked her head and smiled. "Almost anything."

"Come up and change the sheep's water every three or four days? They'll just graze on their own, but they need their water in the blue trough changed a couple of times a week."

"The dog goes and I stay and I tend your sheep, is that the plan?"

"Yeah, well.... So — what do you think? If this Allard guy isn't the killer, who is? And did the innkeeper in Taos see one or two guys check in? Able was out of town just at the time Dennis would have been headed down there. Would your attorney help you run? Yeah, I need to go down."

Down went her third of a glass of red before she spoke. "I don't see why I can't go along. If the dog can go, why can't I?"

"Of course you can go along. But I'd rather have you here with your wonderful antenna upright. We might help each other best by covering the two areas rather than just Taos." I gave her the example of trying to get the feel for what happens now in town with key people, with Peachart, and whether the good citizens of Kootenai Falls buy his explanation for closing down the investigation.

The phone rang then and I let the machine answer it. It was Kate in New York asking that I call her back, saying she had something for me I'd be interested in.

"So what's this Kate person to you?" Amy asked, pouring off the end of the Mouton Cadet.

"We're close," I said.

"How close? As close as we are?"

"I've known Kate for lots of years. I was a kind of mentor to her."

"And plenty more."

"Some day I'll tell you," I said. "For now it's enough to say she's got a life and I have mine. It doesn't change anything between you and me."

There was a beat, and she pursed her lips: "I don't feel like making love tonight, Brew." She looked down into her wine.

"I don't recall bringing it up."

"I mean, I do feel like crawling into bed with you and maybe reading and having another glass of wine and sleeping here next to you."

I didn't know what to say so I covered up and wisecracked: "I'll let you know if I get a better offer."

"You're not disappointed?"

"That a lovely creature wants to crawl into bed with me and sleep here and maybe get up in the morning and have toast and tea with me? Yeah... I'm bitterly disappointed that you don't simply want a sex-and-split evening."

The corners of her lips turned up. She had a way that didn't crowd me, that threw warmth at the log walls, that didn't disturb the feeling of the precious sanctuary of this place that came with the deed. Okay, I said to myself, note this as a warning. Don't get careless, Brewster. Go ahead and be friendly and pop into bed with her. But keep your guard up. Watch out if she leaves a toothbrush somewhere at the top of your medicine cabinet. It's good and warm and free-and-easy now. But watch out, my friend, because that's how many an inroad begins.

Damn that Jiminy Cricket — where is he when you need him?

# Chapter Eighteen

"The thing smells very fishy," Kate was saying the next morning after Amy and I had our tea and she had left for work. "Our stringer says that a few of the local Taos cops went out drinking the night they busted Gordon Allard. They were in something called the Kachina Lounge whooping it up."

I asked if the AP stringer heard anything about a set-up.

"Just that they were overjoyed at finally nailing a guy who's been thumbing his nose at them for a long time."

"Are you going with the Taos story?" I asked.

"We just did a short piece for the inside pages of New Mexico and west Texas papers. Our stringer isn't very experienced in the art of digging."

"I'm going down there. You want me to do something official for you?"

"If you're going anyway, call me with what you get and we'll talk then. But I don't see it having a national appeal. It was different where you are... small town turned up on its ear. But we've done that one."

"What if I told you that some militia types are involved and that the FBI will probably be back into it? Is that enough of a national appeal for the AP?"

She said yes and then we went on to the usual stuff about me being so far away, and why wasn't New York good enough for me....

"You know what would happen if I came back and we were in the same town together?" I said.

"I know. But we were good when you were here, Brew. I didn't feel claustrophobic."

"Neither did I. That was the problem. It was sooner or later going to creep up on us, Wells. You know it."

"Maybe I should come out to Taos," she said.

"If you can swing it." Of course she couldn't so it was easy to say yes. After she had gone through her be-careful routine, I hung up and packed my things and Jessie's food and treats, her best round bed and a new tennis ball.

I called Stenopolis to set up a meeting with her brother then checked my new e-mail box before leaving.

I had six messages from locals welcoming me into the wonderful world of electronic friendship, and a one word message from someone on AOL who went by numbers only. That one word was BACKOFF. Of course it should have been two words. But so far I hadn't seen much use for standard English on the Net.

I opened the back door of the Pathfinder for Jess, who had gained a few pounds and almost missed her jump. She settled down on her bed and we lit out for the road. We quit in Sheridan, Wyoming, where I called Kate again.

"That's a lot of driving for one day," she said.

"We're used to it. We stop a lot and play ball and that helps. The snow is gone except on the Divide."

"So — what time is it in Sheridan?"

"Ten, why?"

"Because it's just after midnight here and I was in bed."

"Alone?" I asked.

"Of course. But I'm due at the office early. So, what's up?"

"I didn't want to take the chance up in Kootenai Falls of telling you about another set of disks. Gil Owen and Dennis developed a program for removing TV advertising. They were getting set to sell it off, entertaining bids."

"The highest bidder being the big networks?"

"Maybe."

"That puts you right in the middle of a shitpot full of danger, my dear idiot." I heard her sigh loudly, as though she had lost patience with her child. "You have the potential of the big money community after you with no friends on your side. Have you considered this?"

"It's hard to imagine American business using hitmen."

"Oh please! What's different between network TV and the Mafia? Not very damned much. Both are pros at playing Monopoly

"Well, what would *you* do? Bring in the cops?"

She sighed deeply, saying something about that's why we pay taxes and why we have an FBI, and so on. "You also might think of your friends back home, Brew. These guys are serious. Whoever is responsible, the truth is that you have four dead people. That's serious."

"I remember," I said, "when those astronauts were blown up in a capsule at the NASA center, Wernher Von Braun was asked on TV for his reaction. He said that wonderful unreconstructed-Nazi line: 'Vell, you know, Ve're not making ize cream.' The same here. I know this isn't ice cream, Wells. But I don't have much choice at this point. Somewhere along the line I'll call that FBI dip."

"If you're not dead first. I keep wondering, Brew — what's in this for you?"

Good question, I decided. "You want the usual answer about justice and morality? Or should I be honest?"

She sighed again, this time loud enough to make her impatience clear.

"Curiosity. I want to see where this leads. I want to find out who is doing all this killing, and who's behind the financing. Aren't you curious? Also, it just messes me all up to see this thing swept under the official carpet."

We said all the good words then and hung up. I had one half glass of Jack Daniel's and watched, alternately, Jay Leno's jaw and David Letterman's gap-toothed sad, phony smile for a few minutes before turning off the TV and lights and going to sleep to the sweet sound of Jessie snoring.

# Chapter Nineteen

I caught up with Dr. Ernest Kassara in the History Department in Boulder at the University of Colorado. He had the disks sitting on a file cabinet in the open. We shook hands, he handed the envelope to me. "This is a very interesting program," he said.

"How so?"

"Simple and uncomplicated — it allows an email sender to send email with an untraceable return address. It lets you do anything on the Internet without divulging your identity or location. A very useful concept for a certain type of individual." Dr. Kassara chuckled. "I take it the disks were meant for illegal situations."

I didn't let on that I had expected something else. This was more like a motive for multiple executions that I could understand. Gil could have been working for those idiot racist groups using the Internet for their PR and organizing strategies. That would explain the FBI's interest. The new laws gave the Feds *carte blanche* in tapping phones and the Internet for terrorist planning, but an absolutely secure communications link the Feds couldn't trace was about as frightening a thing as any federal agency could imagine. Someone could have infiltrated one of the militia and reported on the software project.

I told Kassara that I had no knowledge of who the program was written for but that gruesome events had occurred because of it.

"Well," he said, "in any case, I wash my hands of it. And by the way, Alesandra called a while ago," he said. "She said it was important for you to call her as soon as you can. You can use the phone here if you like."

Dr. Kassara politely left his office while I spoke with his sister. "One more person knows where you are, Brewster," she said in an apologetic tone. "I thought it might be important for Bob Able to know."

"Jesus, you told Able?" With Dennis dead, Able was just another bystander. "Why?"

"He came into town this morning and seemed really upset about Dennis. He said he wanted to get to the bottom of it all, and we just started talking about everything and... it came out."

No point in punishing Stenopolis. But I didn't trust Able. He fit too nicely into the picture of those who might gain from the official books being closed.

"I'm sorry, Brewster. It just slipped out."

"I know," I said. "Be careful now. You know, Able isn't out of the running for bad guy."

"You don't think..."

"He's not out of the running. No one is. Not Able, not any of those assorted Letwiligs, not even the Red Dog girls or Peachart himself. The fact that Peachart was so quick to close the books on this makes one wonder about his motives."

"Oh, you know *him*. He's running for governor."

"Just the same."

The link was clear in my mind as far as motive goes: kill the developers so that the software that makes co-conspirators untraceable is also untraceable. Seems to me that Gil Owen should have been able to figure that out from the start.

Blood under the bridge.

"Another thing," Stenopolis said. "Leo says you should contact someone at a store called Satellite City in Taos. His name is Flip Phillips."

"Like the saxophone player," I said. "We have something in common."

"You do?"

"Inside joke. I'm named after Brew Moore. He was a tenor sax man in San Francisco."

"Anyway... Leo thinks there is something you should know about surveillance equipment in Satellite City stores. He says we had something that the police haven't found yet. Leo said Gil had asked that we invest in this thing, which I have no idea about. Leo says he saw it and that it was something very new on the market to protect one's property, and that there just could be a video tape of the actual murders of Gil and Beth. Oh my God, Brew, what a... perfectly... *hideous* thing to have to see!"

There was that usual expansiveness on Alesandra's part, but this was news to me. I'd been over that place and so had the police. It was hard to imagine that we all missed this new style surveillance stuff. But... maybe. But what an awful find it would be if there were a tape of the crime.

I told her I'd check it out, and then briefly explained about the disks and her brother's assessment... that the program was truly slick and would allow maybe some of those Internet jerks complete anonymity.

"It's possible Gil knew he was working with racist scum bags. But I doubt that Dennis would have known. If he had, he wouldn't have gone on with the project, and he probably would have said something to you about it."

"My god, how on earth did those boys get themselves involved with that kind of person?"

"Two things — money, of course, but also the challenge of doing something like that. Techies don't always think about possible outcomes of they're inventions."

"That must be. I'm just glad I live here so comfortably in the Seventeenth Century, Brewster. I *hate* all of this *hideous* technology. But there's been another development," she said, "Hiram Howell made an offer on the Red Dog."

"Howell did? You're kidding!"

"Leo came in an hour ago and said he offered $260,000 for an outright buy."

I couldn't say as I blamed him. Even with the back room being a crime scene, the Dog was one of the few great businesses in the Kootenai Falls area.

"I hope it doesn't change things too much, that is *if* you sell to him," I said.

"It may not change anything, Brewster. Leo says Howell may not be there all the time, that he might hire someone to run it the way we did."

"If Rita would work for him, she'd be a great manager."

"I don't know her."

"She's worked at the Kootenai Falls Cafe´ forever and lives near the Dog, just up the road from my place," I said.

"Well, we'll see what happens. Leo might decide not to sell after all."

I got back on the road and the sad truth sat heavy in my chest that Gil Owen should have known better than to trust people who want absolute security. Thinking of Gil brought back an old wound, and I shook it off with the driving and by thinking about Jessie, sleeping behind me, perhaps dreaming, riding down the road with the man she loves.

You think in these random threads on a long drive with your dog asleep and sweetly snoring in the back.

Passed Denver and felt bad not stopping to see Ward Dawner, probably the best writer of courtroom mysteries but making considerably less than Grisham. (Saying goes in Kootenai Falls that we have a bookstore: it sells Hallmark cards and John Grisham novels.)

Wanted to see other friends there in Denver as well. Maybe next time. I was focused on finding out how my friend got suckered into all of this sadness.

We turned off I-25 to the southwest at Raton Pass, twisted down through that high country and finally down into a high desert canyon, followed the creek, let Jessie out for a whiz. She went down, stood in the freezing water and looked at the plants. So different from home. She shoved her nose down at the base of dry plants, nosed under rocks. I let her, since it was still too early for snakes. We went on then, slow, nice canyon drive, then a few shacks, an adobe house, the road straightening out, more houses, then finally up into Taos with its many gift shops in the town square, Navajo rugs and silver jewelry, throwback hippy types, and the mandatory young girl with her guitar.

I turned toward the Pueblo, then ahead, the Laughing Horse Inn sign — a large wooden carved and painted horsehead, laughing, Mexican carpets hung near the sign, some in a glass case. Adobe walls framed the place with a narrow drive cut in, and the pile of old adobe structures with a glass-front penthouse perched at the top. A little girl maybe seven sitting on a wood swing told me not to park in front, that her dad doesn't let people park there, that no one else can drive in and park if you stay there. She is Lily, and her dad is Len who came out and greeted me, we shook hands and went inside, Jessie leading us.

"No trouble bringing the dog in?" I asked.

He waved his hand and smiled. "She's beautiful." His smile was like the sun coming up.

# Chapter Twenty

I met Gloria who was sitting at a computer in a five-foot square cluttered office, an upright coffin really, just off the kitchen. She fit right in to the Taos sensibility, with a foot long ponytail and a mild, soft manner about her — a corporate executive dropout, I found out later.

Len introduced me, then opened two Coronas, set them down on the circular kitchen table and gestured to join him. Jessie did a nose tour of the kitchen and back through the foyer and sitting room, pushed her way in to see Gloria, then settled down in the middle of the kitchen for a snooze. She had a way of lying down exactly where everyone coming and going would have to step over her.

"Damnedest thing," Len said. "Nothing like this ever happened while I owned the place. Not a thing. Then I sell to Gloria, and wham, we get a corpse." He tipped the bottle and so did I. First beer of the day. We both said our ahhhhs in unison.

"This is great," I said, looking around.

"A hundred and eleven years old. I'll show you around. By the way, you're staying in the room."

"*The* room?"

"Room five. Where Dennis O'Brien was strangled." He smiled as he said strangled, as though it would become part of the charm of the place. Len is a smallish man with a quick smile and, I found out, quick wit and intelligence, well educated... UCLA, then several very high-paying jobs in construction. Handsome, dark wavy hair, some Hispanic genes floating around in there, he spoke quietly as though we were sitting in the vestibule of a monastery. He also told me later that he wrote screen plays. One thing about B&B innkeepers — they are usually made up of people who have dreamed.

The Laughing Horse actually does resemble a place where monks might have lived, with its open heavy dark beams, stone and Mexican tile floors, adobe walls and many narrow passageways where, as you enter some rooms and some baths, you have to duck to keep from hitting your forehead on a cross beam. Doors of hundred year-old split wood beams, simple locks anyone with determination could force, dark interiors with bright, colorful Mexican carpets.

"So — do they have this Gordon Allard guy still? Has he been charged?" I tipped my bottle up and noticed I had emptied it in four swallows. Len got up to get me another from the small refrigerator in the hallway between the kitchen and Gloria's computer room.

"Haven't heard. I've recently had to kick Gordon out of here three times in one day," Len said. "The last time, he had a bunch of beer bottles surrounding a guest's car, with candles in some of them. He was dancing around the car with a chain saw. He won't take his medicine, and he has these episodes and goes around threatening to kill people."

"So you're glad he's been nailed for this."

"Gordon is a pain in the ass, but he's not a killer. No, I'm not glad. That's just letting the real asshole go free."

"You know that Gordon wouldn't kill?"

"He's crazy, and the police don't like crazy people in a tourist town. Scares off the money people. A couple of your Hollywood types and corporate CEOs have built homes here and out toward the ski area. Someone just bought a whole lot more land out there. Don't want that kind of money scared off. First priority for cops here is maintaining the best PR possible. Taos is safe, Taos is friendly fun. You can let your kids play in the park alone while you shop at the square. That kind of image. It's been bad enough here with the fires, and no snow for the ski seasons. The locals are just hanging on, some of them. So a crazy isn't what they need. But Gordon couldn't have killed him."

"Allard *couldn't* kill Dennis O'Brien?"

"They told me that young man was killed by force. He was garroted in bed, asleep. Gordon doesn't have the reality check to do that. He might sneak in and put lit candles around the guy's bed or something. But garroting is something else."

"You think the police would let me see Gordon?"

"I can fix it," he said, setting my fresh beer before me. Lily came in then and asked if she could read us her latest short story. It was about a man being killed in his sleep by four brown dogs that could talk and that walked around on their hind legs wearing jeans and T-shirts. One of the dogs was the leader because he knew how to climb walls and trees and how to kill people. She is a beautiful little girl with a bright imagination... one of those children you make note of for later on, to check back when they're thirty and famous in the art world. She might well become famous for her beauty, but one could see even at seven that beauty and fame would never be enough for her. She was the kind of child who insisted on substance.

She smiled broadly at her father, holding the sheets of yellow paper out to him. "You can have it," she said. He took them, grabbing at her hand, making her jump back and giggle. She looked at me, then up at the ceiling. "I have another idea," she said, turned and raced back outside, tripping over Jessie.

"Her mother is a musician," Len said. "She does a number of creative things. Lily has always been exposed to the artistic."

It was now dark outside and Len showed me to room five, a twenty-by-ten foot room, red tile floors, open beam ceiling, single bed, wash basin, hooks for clothing. A room lean enough for a Jesuit. The long dark beams went the length of the room, with what Len called *latillas* filling the spaces between them. The foot-long, skinned aspen branches about two inches thick look like round ladder steps too close together. A fine ceiling for an adobe-walled Jesuit's chamber.

"Jessie has her own bed," I told him, hoping she was welcome to spend the night. He just smiled, showed me the low beam of the washroom across the narrow hallway.

"Someone told me film people stay here regularly."

He smiled again. "In the penthouse. It's big enough for entertaining. Room five is too small."

Back out in the kitchen I said that we all thought that Dennis was on his way to Arizona, that he was a Hopi and was headed home fast. I told Len why.

"We talked some," he said, "and Dennis was no Hopi. He was already home. He was a Anasazi; some of his family still live here in the Pueblo. Well," he said, "they claim to be direct descendants of the Anasazi." He explained that Hopi and Navajo tribes also descended from Anasazi, which means *ancient ones*. "Current wisdom has it that climate conditions changed so drastically that the Anasazi who were left drifted into the high country and ultimately built the pueblo communities. Dennis stayed here with us because he felt safer in the closed in area here. But he also had to wait until the leaders at the Pueblo would admit him. It's complicated because you get your own place, and there isn't always room for people who once lived there to come back home."

"Did you know Dennis before?" I asked. It seemed to me that Len knew a lot about him for just offering a safe room.

"No. One of the elders from the Pueblo came over and talked with me for a while about what was going on. Dennis had showed up on the Pueblo doorstep asking to be let in."

"I see."

"He also needed a telephone," Len added. "There are no phones, no electricity, no wells or running water out there. It's really inconvenient for a lot of Indians who work in Taos. I know an attorney out there and a shop owner, and you can never get them except by driving out to the Pueblo. But Dennis had to have a phone, he told me. I guess to keep up to date about the situation in Montana.

"Well, I wonder about something else that went along with the crime scenes up in Montana. Do the pueblo Indians have eagle feather or peyote rituals?"

"Only the Hopis are allowed to take golden eagles for their ceremonies. Some use peyote here at times, but very few. It's extremely personal, and not condoned by the leaders. Why?"

I explained about the pieces of peyote buttons found at one of the crime scenes and the scattering of a few eagle feathers. "That was roughly Hopi-style stuff, right?"

"Some white man's idea of the Hopi," he said. "Even those over in Arizona who use peyote don't do it outside of where they live. It's a very personal thing, not like marijuana. Only the white man thinks it is because that's the way the white man uses it. Peyote isn't a recreational drug for American Indians."

Len was well read about the Anasazi ability to maintain the old ways... no electricity, no running water... a free set of rooms in the Pueblo for anyone of the nation who chose to live there.

"Well," I said, "this is why I came down here. You know, when the prosecutor up in Montana found out about Dennis' murder and that the Taos police had an open and shut case against a suspect, he closed the books. It's information like this that could get the thing re-opened."

The beer was light and icy and I could feel myself heading for a night of it. I didn't want to. I wanted to think. I wanted to get to bed and let the road seep out of my muscles, down my back, legs, out through the heels of both feet. I could tell Len was winding down, ready to gather up Lily and head home for the night. But I was just beginning. The icy beer, a lighter feeling, all that meant a fine and deep undisturbed sleep — for a change.

In bed in the tiny room where Dennis had died, I tried thumbing through the new *New Yorker*, looking at the cartoons. Nothing was funny, not even Booth. So I let my mind rumble with wonderings about why I was so concerned about someone like Dennis who I knew but not well. Am I this concerned about justice? Before I got to an answer, Jessie was snoring, lying on her side on her bed. I hoped I'd sleep like that, but my mind was jumping around: there must be many, many murderers walking around free today, with no worries about being found out. You wonder, at night, just how many killers go on living good lives. You wonder this in a room where agony occurred.

# Chapter Twenty-One

I tried to catch Amy before she took off for the office but only got her answering machine. I wanted to check on what was happening — if anything — and tell her where I'd be. But — no Amy, and I didn't want to call in at the paper.

I had a quiet cup of coffee with Gloria in the kitchen, then Jessie and I headed down to the county lockup. No problem getting to see this Allard fellow, Len had greased the way. Just sign in and they get his permission, then you meet in a tiny interview room.

Gordon Allard walked into the visitor's room and sat at the table across from me. He grinned, put his hands on the table and looked at the ceiling. He was a small man with explosive, blondish hair going gray and a snarl of a blondish beard, two inch-wide vertical gray streaks on either side of his mouth. In a blue suit and red tie he would be a commanding, if jockey-sized, presence, except for the unkempt beard. I'd heard from Len that Allard had a terrible upbringing, that his parents saw his extraordinary intelligence as plain weird. He was institutionalized in his teens and there is talk that as a pre-schooler he had killed a playmate — beat her to death on the back lawn of his home amid all of his lead toy soldiers that had been placed around the yard in defensive positions, as though waiting for the little girl to attack. It is rumored that the little girl made fun of Allard, picking up several soldiers and throwing them over a nearby fence. A transgression indeed, but she paid for it with her life. Or so they said.

Since then and since his time in the funhouse, Allard had gone from that bad to far worse. Now, Len said, on his bad days when he won't take his medicine, he drives around in an old station wagon decorated with yellow, pink and black symbols, arrows, cartoon characters, and various shoes hanging by ties from this or that knob on the car. The shoes he finds along the road. Whenever he spots a shoe, he stops, grabs it and says elaborate prayers over it and the missing foot, then ties it to his station wagon and speeds off.

Cars, trucks — vehicles of any kind — seem at the center of his universe and fantasies. Putting beer cans around one, and lit candles, and his Indian-style dances around them with chain saw held high — all of that makes perfectly good sense to him. No wonder the local police were pleased to grab him as a murder suspect.

"No notion," Allard said, his arms out as if trying to stop the spinning earth. His face was broad as a pie tin, eyes little more than slits, and ears that seemed upside down.

I asked him what was no notion.

"Man...," he said, "you wouldn't believe. No notion. No notion whatsoever."

"What wouldn't I believe, Gordon?"

His eyes moved to the right as though he were listening to a secret conversation in the room next door. After a moment, he said, "Put it this way," he said, then pressed his hands together in a kind of Buddhist gesture of greeting.

I asked how he was being treated, but he did not answer. He turned his head away.

"Are you taking your Lithium now, Gordon?" I asked.

No answer.

I sat for a few minutes, then said, "I know you're taking it now, so let's just talk. I'm not in any way involved with why you're here. You understand that, don't you?"

He stood then and moved away from the table, hands out as though he were about to do the Zorba dance. He held it for a moment, then snapped his head toward me and smiled open mouthed.

"Where is this getting us, Gordon? Are you just trying to show me you're crazy? You're not crazy, Gordon. You and I know that."

"Two plus two is four," he said, coming back to the table. He stood over me for a few moments, then collapsed into the chair, slouching, kicking his legs out, dropping his arms to his side. All the air went out of his body.

"Two plus two," I repeated. I was ready to leave.

"Four plus four is eight." He sat up. "Eight plus eight is sixteen... only sometimes," he said, pointing at me. "And sometimes the correct answer is four. Now that's crazy." His arms flew up from his sides. "Eight plus eight is sixteen and sometimes it's four."

He looked at the ceiling, arms above him as if beseeching the gods. "People go by that." Arms back down. "They go by twelve plus twelve is twenty-four and twelve plus twelve is twelve. And it isn't... NUTS."

"What are you saying. I'm not following," I said. I studied his features. There were hardly any lines on his face and none on his forehead. I read somewhere — maybe it was Dostoevski, maybe it was Scott Fitzgerald — that the mentally ill seem all to look so young, to not age, as though their minds on vacation did not use up their bodies as quickly as the rest of us. Allard had that perennial child's skin. Only on a near middle-aged man it was more frightening than attractive.

He went on for a while, zigzagging between ideas, and then clamming up. He'd start something, then put his hand over his mouth like a child who had just realized he'd said a bad word.

"Don't play nuts, Allard," I said finally. "If anything, I'm on *your* side. I just need to know a few things that you know about the night Dennis O'Brien was murdered."

"Look at your watch," he said.

"All right," I said. "So — now what?"

"Your watch tells you what? It tells you twelve plus nine equals what? Nine, right? Hands of a clock. A twelve-base system right in the middle of a ten-base world. Am I right?"

I nodded. He had me and I gave in. I was ready to just forget it. "Gordon," I said finally, "will you help me?"

"Cow one is not cow two."

Here we go again. "Gordon...."

"I learned that."

"I need you to focus for me for just a few minutes."

"From a book by an Indian. But the picture on the jacket cover was of a Japanese man. Then I read he was born in Canada. Crazy? He says cow one isn't cow two. Don't be so quick to judge cow-ness. So — from a Canadian with Japanese eyes I find out cow one isn't cow two."

He folded his arms. Body language said, "That's all, folks." I read his body language. He had closed me off.

The Canadian was, of course, S. I. Hayakawa, writer and professor of semantics and former U.S. Senator from California. So — was he crazy? Quoting Hayakawa?

"Tell me about the night of the murder," I said.

He squinted at me, lips pursed, arms still folded across his chest. Finally, he relaxed his arms. "I go by ten-base time, man" he said. "Same as money. I don't dig that code switching shit."

"Gordon...."

He unfolded his arms, and his shoulders sagged slightly. He smiled. There was a quick twinkle in his eye, as though he realized I understood his game. He was an actor. He liked the attention. And he was also tracking pretty well.

"Yeah, I'm taking the pills now. I didn't have the money

before. They give them to me in here."

"Were you at the Laughing Horse on that night? I'm thinking along the lines that you were set up."

He nodded. "For a while. Then the cops came. Been trying to get me in here for a year now. I didn't kill nobody. I know it, they know it."

"Why do you think they arrested you?"

"Because I'm crazy. I know it, they know it, the town knows it. Being crazy and dancing Indian dances in public places isn't a crime. It just bothers them."

"You know all that?"

"I'm crazy, I'm not blind."

"So you know what's going on."

"More than some."

"About that night... can you tell me what went on?"

He squinted at me again. "I'm reading Camus. You ever read Camus?"

I told him I had.

"*The Stranger*, I'm reading that now, in here. Passes the time."

He stood up then and stretched, paced across the room and back, then sat down again. "I was at the Laughing Horse. Len sat with me. We had a couple of Keystone Lights I brought him. He likes Corona. I like Keystone."

"Focus now, Gordon. I need your help."

"Anyway, we had just a couple. Nothing much because I was taking my medicine again for my bipolar. That stuff doesn't mix with alcohol. Not that I care much, and then...."

"So you were taking your Lithium."

"And then I packed up and drove down to the Kachina. That jazz trio that plays in there... the drummer is the leader, and he's a funny guy and a friend of mine. And I wanted to talk the bargirl out of getting married.

"So this guy approaches me, tells me he'll give me money to show up at the Laughing Horse at two A.M. I follow instructions according to *his* watch, not mine. There was four-hundred dollars at stake. Even a nutzy can manage well with a dose of Lithium and a few hundred dollars.

"So I go to the Inn and the police are there."

I asked him what the guy with the roll of hundreds looked like.

"Dude. Short, pointy face, thick wallet. I call him Red because he had this red car."

"Red car as in a red Mercedes?"

"A red Mercedes, to be exact."

"A convertible?"

"A convertible. Yes, a convertible."

"It's important, Gordon. Try to remember."

"A red Mercedes convertible."

"Was the guy named Bob?"

"Didn't have a name. NoName was his name." He giggled.

# Chapter Twenty-Two

I phoned Amy. "Bob Able *was* down here with Dennis," I said. "Our resident manic depressive described him down to the red convert." I was calling from a pay phone at a Quick Stop, but Amy was in the office and I was aware that she had to be careful. Tom didn't take well to his employees wasting time on the phone with deadbeats and closed murder cases.

"Could be coincidence. A lot of people have red cars."

"I know I know I know. But maybe we can get Able to tell us he was here, and maybe even why."

"How you gonna do that, Kimosabi?"

"I'll ask him, just confront him straight out."

"And when he says no?"

"I'll tell him I have a witness who says he made a deal with him. Then I'll ask him what he was doing down there."

"And he'll say he was protecting his client. No, Brew, that won't prove anything. And you don't really think Bob Able could commit murder, do you?"

"I wonder."

"Because Kellog Letwilig was supposedly out of town at one of those militia training camps learning how to be a merc. And he's a lot more likely candidate to be able to do that kind of work than Mr. Clean Attorney is."

"Maybe. Do you *know* Kellog was at that camp? All the time? How is Peachart handling the PR about him closing the case? Any reverberations in the community?"

"Not from the paper. Tom says it's not our business. I talked with a few of the locals like two of the doctors at the clinic, and that woman who lives on Seeley where you nearly got clobbered by Hiram Howell. Neither Doc Wes or Doc Pete have an official opinion, and the woman says its business-as-usual by the Peachart-for-Governor folks."

"Who's this woman?"

"Someone you don't know and I do. She lives a few blocks

up from me. She's got this cute little daughter. Very bright, both of them. But she's lived in Kootenai Falls most of her life except for a bunch of years in Seattle. She knows the ins and outs, and the gossip at the Red Dog is that Peachart knows he's not fooling any locals, he just wants the books clean so it looks good statewide. He knows he wouldn't get many votes out of Kootenai Falls anyway, because they know him too well. But there aren't that many voters in Kootenai Falls anyway. He's counting on a clean look as prosecutor and the quick kill on this case to launch him into the seat in Helena. Next stop, the U.S. Senate."

"All that from the Red Dog?"

"You know how it works — you want to know something, you go to the john in the Dog and ask."

"Pretty good for the new girl in town. And, sweet new girl, did you know that Hiram Howell has come up with a $260,000 offer to buy the Dog?"

"I did hear that... from Rita in the Cafe´. Who'd you hear it from?"

"Stenopolis herownself," I said. "What do you think?"

"I think they should take the money and run."

"I hate to see that asshole get in there. You'd have to deal with him all the time."

"Well... don't go there."

"Right," I said. "It's my home away from cabin."

I told her to see if she could find a Kalispell PI we both knew who worked for the newspaper now and then. "I will check out down here where Able went and stayed, make sure of it, get the dates, his whole trail. But we need to know about all three of the Letwiligs. Tell the PI he gets his normal fee if he does the work in a few days. I especially want to know about Kellog and where Lamar was."

"You're going to have to tell me more, Brewster. If I'm Tonto, I don't want to be left out of anything critical."

"You'll know, don't worry. I just don't want to do it now on the phone. I'll be back in a few days. I can prove a motive that can reopen the case, no matter what Peachart wants."

"Do you miss me, Moore?" she asked.

"If you'll tell me my sheep are fine and that you've watered them, I'll answer you."

"They're fine and I've watered them. So — ?

"No," I said and laughed. "But I miss my sheep."

"I think I've just fallen in hate with you, Moore," she said.

In the afternoon I checked with the Best Western-Kachina desk clerk who seemed not to understand the confidentiality factor about motel registrations. She was probably still in high school, working part-time and had no investment one way or another in proper policy. She was tall with a wrinkled forehead and completely bewildered by my questioning. She just shrugged and took my request as an order to look up Able's dates. And there he was, his signature on the card, the dates, in on May 4th, out on the 7th, and the total — $422.87, including a hefty Kachina bar tab.

I then spent two hours out at the Pueblo, part of the time talking to a girl who runs the Summer Rain, a silver jewelry gift shop. She introduced me to a tribal elder with a ubiquitous surname. It seemed almost everyone in the Pueblo was either "Smith" or "Petees," so to speak.

The elder said that no one had been buried in the Pueblo cemetery for months, and that no ashes have come into the compound. The fact was that Dennis O'Brien had not entered his former Pueblo home area dead or alive. I asked then about peyote.

"Peyote is a long time ago," he said. "Years ago you would wait a long while before your instruction was complete, and then you would look down at the plant and study it, and then you would go into the flower."

"Into the flower?"

"A saying we have, but also a real experience. I've never had it, and I do not hold with peyote." Smiling then, he said, "I am more the Jim Beam kind. I go into the kiva and sweat it out after and feel better. Peyote is confusion."

I asked about eagle feathers, and he confirmed it was only Hopi who used them. They were allowed to take four golden eagles this past year for their feathers.

We sat together on an adobe slab next to their river where they still draw water that is pure and that runs all year long even in this high desert, and this small creek ran down from their sacred mountain and through their land, pure and still untouched by the contemporary world.

I finally stood and said I'd be going and thanked the man who, I was told, was a kind of war lord but without wars to fight. "I am old now and covered with my life," he said, then added, "a great man here said that once — Ben Marcus. His real name was Red Willow Dancing." He looked up at the sky. "I am old as well, which is a privilege denied my ancestors. A few centuries ago, old for an Indian was forty. I am nearly ninety. That is a mystery I cannot understand. I also have no understanding of why Dennis O'Brien was coming home. Why he was murdered is not a question for us because we no longer knew him. You must know some-one well to know his enemies."

Then the old man said he had some advice for me. "Do not go so fast through your life," he said. "Do not overrun your shadow."


I met with Len and he introduced me to his wife, Sylvia, who is the kind of woman I would have expected him to marry— the kind often described as having mature beauty. Dark-eyed, a smile filled at both corners with secrets. They were the kind of couple that, if he were alive today, Henry James would be writing about. Delicate, artistic royalty merged with classic features and, as Scott Fitzgerald wrote, "...the fresh look of many clothes."

I told them I would be heading back north and we said our good-byes, and I took yet another new story from Lily who told me she wrote it for me to read in the motel so I'd have some manner of entertainment.

I drove down toward the crossroads and then to the Satellite City store just south of the center of town.

It turned out that Flip Phillips is the *manager* of the Taos Satellite City. It also turned out that she is a handsome woman with a gray-streaked boyish buzz haircut and steel-colored eyes that swung at you like a friendly double-barreled 12 gauge Winchester.

I asked her about what Leo had meant about having something the police wouldn't have found. It was new surveillance equipment, I said, and Flip knew exactly what I meant. She showed me the usual cameras on the ceilings in several corners that were used to help prevent shoplifting. She said those particular cameras were dummies.

"They were all we had until this new technology came in. Some of the franchises had the opportunity to buy into it at a good discount before we began selling them to our customers. We also sell various other sophisticated systems from that same manufacturer."

A black mantel clock hardly twelve inches tall sat on top of one of the TVs in the stack area — a wall of thirty or forty televisions all tuned to the same channel showing a thin, grinning Oprah draped in an overstuffed chair, mike in hand, talking with Harrison Ford, who sat stiffly, as if chained to the matching leather chair beside her. Forty Oprahs, forty Harrison Fords. Such is the modern day wallpaper of the electronics store.

"It just looks like a modern clock for a mantel, right?" Phillips said. "But look." She picked it up and held it up for me to look at. "This is just an empty box with a transmitter inside the size of a 9 volt battery. The clock works are about the size of a half dollar."

"Where's the camera and lens?" I asked.

Pointing, she said, "See that tiny piece of metal and glass at the center of the nine?" The round piece of glass, obviously the lens, was smaller than a contact lens. "That's it. And it's a kind of fisheye. Takes in most of a room, but they've worked out the distortion you use to get years ago. The camera is motion-sensitive and takes a still every few seconds, so that you get the images and a continuum of action. It transmits a black and white image to a mini-VCR up to two-thousand feet away, or with satellite, an unlimited distance from the camera. Some of them you get in catalogs transmit only about three-hundred feet. With this one, you can tape for 24 hours, then you go rewind or save it. The tape is that audio cassette tape size. It also takes a key to open the recording unit. It's designed like those black boxes that aircraft use. Indestructible. They sell this in the very upscale Topix sales catalog. That catalog also sells a camera on a strap that looks like a wrist watch. It costs two-thousand dollars."

"That's really astounding equipment if it works," I said. "It could be anywhere and you'd have to know about it to notice it."

"This is a second generation," she said. "The first recording unit had to be on a sight line with the transmitter and, as I said, not more than two-thousand feet distance between the two. This next generation can work from two small satellite dishes — an up-and down link. But it's expensive; it's for very large areas with many cameras with the VCR receptor at some central control point. It was developed for the military."

"It's so small, we all easily missed it," I said mostly to myself. I guess we weren't looking for a clock.

"Missed it?" she asked. "Do you know someone who has this product?"

"At crime scene... back in Montana. I wondered if this kind of equipment might have been installed."

I asked if she thought a back room store the size of the one in Kootenai Falls would have gone for a purchase this expensive.

"This one without the satellite connection is six-hundred dollars, and it cuts theft insurance costs so that payback will come quickly. Yeah," she said, "I'll bet they went for it."

"How much for this new generation with the dishes?"

"Add another thousand, plus the T-1 satellite connection. But you can hook up with a long-distance carrier like MCI for that for a couple of hundred a month."

Just protecting cash receipts from the Red Dog wouldn't justify that outlay. But Gil was protecting a lot more than that. It wasn't hard to imagine Gil footing most of the bill for the Satellite-based equipment and lying to Leo and Alesandra about the cost.

Flip smiled and asked if I was a detective.

"Journalist," I said, and her smile broadened.

I left quickly, before she had time to announced that she had always wanted to write.

I called Stenopolis.

"Tell Leo not to let anyone into that back room," I said. "No one except Amy Kroll. I'm going to send her on an errand, so please give her a key. She's going to be looking for that surveillance equipment," I said. I added: "Any news about the sale to Howell yet?"

"Not yet, but Leo says he wants it and it's just a matter of getting the price right. So — I'll see that Amy gets a key. But my dear boy, *why...* should Leo trust... *any*one? He doesn't trust the back of his hand, you know."

It was always a pleasure to hear her bravado manner. It made me feel important, as though I were an entire audience. "I know I know I know," I said. "But this is really important that not even Peachart gets in."

"My dear, neither Leo nor I trust anyone except ourselves and you. And we trust *Vreeland... Peachart* least of all. Not to worry. I'll let Amy have the key. Leo says that camera and surveillance tape should still be there. He says Dennis and Gil put it in just before the, uh, *terrible....* Well, not to dwell on that. I wonder, do you think Greta's safe here? You know that nothing's changed. We still have the cloud of a killer over our heads, even if the police don't want to admit it."

"If she's not seen, they'll think she's in hiding somewhere out of town, which would be natural."

Stenopolis agreed. "Oh... I *do* wish she were."

"So do I."

I placed a call to Amy and gave her specific instructions to get the Red Dog's back room key from Leo and look for a Dick

Tracy-style surveillance system. I described the clock and told her that if she found it and it was too hard to disconnect that she should leave it in place.

"Gee," she said. "I'll bet our friendly officials would love to know about that kind of equipment."

"You tell them and you're a dead woman," I said.

"Literally," she said.

"And make sure you're not followed."

Jessie settled down after a few minutes as we rolled out of town and snaked through the canyon back toward the high country leading into Colorado. It was good to be on the road again with my dog. A warmish wind blew around inside making Jessie's fur flutter. But... something wasn't right back there. My conversation with that old man at the Pueblo... something was missing there. No live Dennis had appeared, so where was Dennis' body?

I hadn't finished snooping yet. When I turned back, Jess stood and looked at me in the rearview mirror. "Gotta go back, girl. You and I... we totally missed something."

All the way back to town she had her head out of the driver's side back window, eyes narrowed, grinning at the wind. I thought then: what have I done right in my life to deserve this lovely creature?

# Chapter Twenty-Three

At the county morgue I asked the deputy coroner for the paper-work on Dennis. "Is the body still here?" I asked.

"Cremated. Couple days ago right after he is brought in. No waiting, no fuss. In out. He is ashes right off the bat. Quick like a bunny. No muss, no fuss."

"Without any family sign-off? Is that legal?"

"Cremated's all I know, fella. You want more, then you want another person who is not me. You want to see the coroner about this person who is now ashes. Are you family?"

"I'm a reporter, I want to see the paperwork." This old deputy coroner was a strange little guy, maybe in his early sixties with slicked-back gray hair and a hard look in his eyes as though he's seen plenty enough of death. A sallow skin exactly right for the kind of deep basement work he does.

"Who for?" he said.

"Who for what?"

"Who for are you a reporter for? What's your newspaper?"

Figuring Tom Everett would cover for me in a pinch, I just told him it is a Kootenai Falls bi-weekly.

"Never heard of it in my life," he said, opening a drawer. "I thought maybe you were from *The Denver Post*. Or maybe a Santa Fe or Albuquerque paper... some paper which I, being the coroner's helper, had heard of. I was at one time a bigshot editor a long time ago and one time I heard of a lot of newspapers and magazine companies and book companies because of what I was a long time ago but am not no longer, having been knifed squarely in the back one fine day. What's the name of the Kootenai Falls paper that I never heard of?"

"*The Mountain Inquirer*."

He placed the open ledger on the desk between us and spun it around so that it faced me.

"Montana," he said. "You got a lot of snow in Montana. You got a lot of weather up there in Montana which it is cold all the time, and your heating costs a small fortune and you spend all your money on trying to stay warm with heavy coats and long underwear. Who would live in Montana where it is nine months cold? Here's the name you want," he said, pointing. "In out, just like I said."

"In and out?"

"In out. He comes in, he goes out... to the ovens. Why? Don't ask, because I'm just working here making for myself a living having formerly been knifed in the back out of my major life's profession with no hope of returning to said noble profession because of said knifing. So, to be specifically clearly up front and kosher about it, he, being the O'Brien of which you and I speak, comes in, goes out. In out. They cook him. So? — dead is dead."

He put on a full-length brown coat over his white smock. "It's cold nine months of the year up there in Montana. Just talking about it makes for me a shiver."

"It's cold *twelve* months of the year down here. This is a freezer," I said.

"Yeah... but nice in summer."

The ledger entry showed that one Dennis Albert O'Brien had indeed arrived, was put on a slab, rolled into the wall of slabs in the ice box. "Death by strangulation." Time and date of delivery, height and weight of the corpse, scars noted, personal effects listed as "wallet/ID," signature of Grace T. Selway, M.D. Signatures of law enforcement officers delivering the body where Jerry Cauldfield and a scribbled Sgt. John Foster, both with TPD entered after their signatures.

"So what are you reporting on here? Dead is dead, so what's the story? It's not a story I would myself individually and personally go out of my way to read about in the Taos newspaper, so why do they go out of their way to read such a story as this one is in a Montana newspaper?"

"They don't read it, they use the paper to light their wood stoves."

He chuckled and waved his hand. "At least you gotta good sense of humor, kid. Most people come down here aren't looking to be in their sense of humor. Where you from, kid? I mean where you from originally?"

"Oakland."

"Oakland," he repeated. "I never met anybody from Oakland."

"That's because when you ask somebody from Oakland where they're from they always tell you San Francisco."

"To tell you the truth, Mr. Oakland, I never see no body come in here with this paperwork. I mean, since you have this Oakland sense of humor, I can lay it on the line to you. In my own personal knowledge, there was no dead person attached to this entry we have before us." He folded the ledger and slid it back into place in the file drawer. "That's not at all in any way, shape or form to be saying they couldn't have rolled him in here after I was gone or looking the other way, because, of course, they could have done just that simple thing when, as I say, I was gone or looking the other way and not here looking right here by this desk which is officially incoming. But I saw no O'Brien with my own eyes, which isn't something that happens every day or night of the year around here in the Taos morgue."

"But all of these signatures?"

"I don't see no doctor here, only police. I don't see no corpse here, only police. Plenty police, not so plenty doctors or corpses with the name tag O'Brien. So who signs for the doctor? Hello? I don't see the coroner here neither. Say, you ought to go see the coroner about this matter so you get your story straight. He's plenty helpful to the newspaper people because his job is an elected slot which depends on he has to be friendly or perhaps for sure he is suffering the consequences later at the polls. But there is more story in some body not coming in here dead than there is in coming in here being dead. One is usual, the other is not so usual. In my book," he said, waving his hand, "dead is dead... but to be dead, you gotta show up."

I thanked him and we shook hands. Funny little guy with a funny way about him. He says everything the longest way around and with the most clichés he can think of. He could have been a standup comic, but I guess he liked basement freezers better than crowds.

Across the street at the Taos Police Department, detectives Cauldfield and Foster were tied up they said, busy, not available for at least an hour, maybe more. So I looked up the office of Dr. Grace. T. Selway, signer of death certificates.

Her practice was housed in a traditional adobe office building just off the city square. The waiting room was decorated in contemporary east Indian, with small prayer rugs hanging on the walls among photographs of Gandhi and Franklin Roosevelt and one of the many Gorman American Indian women sitting amid their flame-colored skirts, making pots.

The receptionist wore a white smock over a sari, and spoke with that clipped east Indian by-way-of-Britain accent. "Do you have an appointment?" she asked, not looking down at her appointment book nor at me.

"It's about a death certificate she signed. I'm a reporter following up a story about a murder here in Taos. I'd like to see

Dr. Selway for maybe ten minutes at the most."

The woman rose gracefully, and without the look of motion went back into the bowels of the office and I heard a crushed rustling sound of her starched white smock and whoosh of her sari..

She returned and handed me a scrap of paper on which there was written a telephone number. "Dr. Selway is sorry that she can't see you, but she asked me to have you call this number."

I caught a glimpse of the good doctor moving between rooms and took a chance: "Dr. Selway! There was no body connected to your death certificate. O'Brien. Dennis O'Brien?" She stopped in the corridor and looked first at the receptionist who shrugged, the palms of her hands facing the ceiling.

"Did you see a body? You signed the certificate!"

There were three people in the waiting room busily reading *National Geographic*.

The door to the inner sanctum opened with Dr. Grace standing at the doorway, one hand on her hip, which said clearly that one of us was in deep shit.

In her office she pointed at one of the leather chairs on the patient side of the desk. No words, just a bony finger telling me exactly all I needed to know.

"You're from Kootenai Falls?" she said, her eyes narrowed.

I told her I was. "I'm a reporter."

"From Kootenai Falls," she said as colorless as a possible, as though it had never occurred to anyone that a reporter might actually be from Montana.

"Indeed. All the way from Kootenai Falls, following Dennis O'Brien." I hoped I was showing some impatience. "Why do you ask?"

"Do you know someone named Russell Pace?"

Why did I feel as though I were about to get my rights read to me?

"I know him. He's a CIA agent."

"FBI," she corrected.

"Whatever."

"The number my receptionist handed you is his. You're to call him."

"Dr.... whatever your name is...."

"Selway."

You do that thing... "forgetting" your interviewee's name, when you want to let her know she isn't important enough for you to recall her name. But you do it in such a way as to not allow the subject to have a complaint against you for being rude.

"I'm here to try to figure out what happened to a very nice young man who I've known for years who has been railroaded for murder up where I live."

"I understand."

"Oh you *do,* do you? Well, I get a run-around from the local police and a deputy coroner who is half crazy who says there was no body, and now you."

She sighed deeply then. "All you people are working at cross purposes, and I'm getting very tired of it."

I asked her to explain.

"I'm sorry but I cannot. Not in specific terms. I *can* tell you though that the man whose death certificate I signed — by mutual agreement between the FBI and the local sheriff, I might add — is not dead."

There was the bombshell I'd been hoping for.

"He is under government protection," she continued. "I can tell you this because you'd figure it out sooner or later anyway. But I must also caution you to go no further in your own investigation until you talk with Mr. Pace. The death at the Laughing Horse Inn is not your affair."

"We're calling it a death are we?"

"Officially it's a murder by strangulation."

"Well, Dr. Selway, I understand why I'm not supposed to be a shit disturber here. But I hope *you* understand that I am under no obligation, ethically, morally or otherwise, to back off. Dennis O'Brien, wherever the poor slob is, is not guilty of murder, and I mean to prove it. Also, there are three formerly living human beings up there in Montana who are no longer with us. I mean to have their a day in court. And whatever the obstacles, whatever the motives of our government, there are some simple human values involved here."

"And there are some very complex human values involved in my signing that death certificate."

"Oh, I don't fault you, and I don't really care to understand or complain about the FBI or its motives. Neither should you wish to obstruct my research. And there is really one more very important thing here."

"And that is?"

"My border collie has been sitting in my car for the past two hours, and I think she has to pee. So — I'll be going now... to let my dog pee, and get back on the road out of town. I'd appreciate it if you would tell Russell Pace, and whoever else comes along asking, that I have no intention of backing down. I'm going to find out what's going on, and I'm going to have the homicide cases reopened. You can tell them when they come calling that I have new evidence of who the murderer is in Kootenai Falls and, more important, it's all too obvious why our benevolent government officials want this Laughing Horse murder closed down. You can tell them all of that for me."

The dry high desert air outside filled me with fresh resolve. It also filled me with a false sense of security. I had been neglecting my back when I drove to the town park where Jessie could run around and do her marking thing. It didn't occur to me that I might have been followed leaving Selway's office.

# Chapter Twenty-Four

The May desert sun was on our backs as Jessie loped out into the grass following a scent trail, probably a squirrel's. After a good long squat and a few markings, she was off examining a pile of sand-colored stones when suddenly she spun back toward me, raised her ears and seemed to stand on her toes, tail high over her back, her eyes flashing in the late afternoon light.

"Mr. Moore," the voice said from behind me. "Can we..." He didn't get the rest of the sentence out before Jessie was standing between the two of us facing him. Her teeth were not bared, but there was no mistaking her stance: she was saying in herding dog body language that this intruder was a threat to me and that he may not wish to take one small step forward.

"Mr. Moore, call off your dog. I don't want to hurt him."

"He's a she, and I'm not sure that's the way it would play out." Jess' ears lowered as though she understood me, then she lowered her head lowered and a heavy jet aircraft rumble of a growl came from deep within her chest.

"Mr. Moore, I don't want to hurt your dog."

"I assure you if you do try that she'll have your throat in her digestive tract before you can draw your pistol. So just take a few steps backward, slowly."

"We need to talk," he said backing away.

Jessie went into her "down," watching closely.

"I'll be the judge of that."

"Please call your dog off, Mr. Moore."

"That'll do, Jess," I said. She stood and trotted back to me and sat, thoroughly pleased with herself but ready for the next assignment. She stretched, chin to the sky, then settled at my feet.

"The murder at the Laughing Horse Inn wasn't a death at all, was it, Mr...?

"Crampton. John Crampton." He rolled out his FBI ID.

"It wasn't a murder, it's a cover up. And you're going to tell me what it's covering up."

I motioned toward a picnic table and we went over, Jessie ahead, looking for other dog's messages and squirrels.

"You're right about the death here. But there are good reasons for what we're doing. There is a serious matter of national security involved."

"What serious matter?"

"And if you continue to be an obstruction, we may be forced to legally restrain you."

Crampton seemed almost trustworthy, for a federal agent. Maybe it was time to listen.

"We can bring you in on this in a general way. But it's not for publication. Any leakage here and there is big jail time ahead."

I nodded. Gentleman's agreements are done like cards — close to the chest. This is macho country and we must all pretend to be Clint Eastwood in order to communicate. In that way, talking to the FBI was like talking to Jim Letwilig.

"There is reason to curtail the investigation in Kootenai Falls, Mr. Moore. There is a sensitive situation there and more disruption would cause system dysfunction. We have someone there we are protecting."

*System dysfunction.* You just gotta love these guys.

"Someone more important that the Owens," I said, "and that Okla woman, obviously. Someone important enough so that we have to sidestep justice."

"It's done all the time, in one way or another."

"I know."

"Murderers go free, other serious crimes go unpunished. Much more frequently than you might suspect."

I had to agree that it happened all the time. "However, Mr. Crampton, wouldn't it be nice if someday, like for instance today, we all decided not to play it that way anymore? Not to violate the spirit of the land, not to cast a bucket of piss on the graves of our dear departed? Maybe now is a good time to start fresh and say that we all will try to search out the guilty and that the guilty will not be let go because of a higher value placed on politics or whatever you're placing that higher value on today."

Crampton went on: "The man we're protecting in Kootenai Falls has the ability to seriously embarrass the United States. He is not involved in what went on there, the deaths I mean, except in a very peripheral way. He's not the murderer of those three people, as far as we know. But further tampering with evidence and motives and such as that will ultimately divulge this man's identity. And I can tell you now, right here where there are no witnesses, that the U.S. intelligence community has no intention of letting that happen."

He stood up and smiled down at me for emphasis, the smile used as a threat. Jessie's head rose sharply, ears up. "We know about the software for untraceable communication. We know about the purchase and who the buyers are. None of that nor the determination of who killed the Owens and Ms. Lynette Okla, is important enough to pursue at the cost of revealing who the man is we are protecting, or why. I hope you understand, because we are doing you the unique favor here of warning you to let it go. I'm speaking for Russell Pace, Mr. Moore. He has been a close observer of the whole situation and is the agent in charge of making it work for our interests. Any threat to those interests will result in what we call a situation to be neutralized. We have removed such threats in the past, and we will do so again."

He squared his shoulders. His eyes narrowed and he nodded once. "I trust you understand. There is no middle ground here."

In the motel that night I first called Kate. I needed the name of that source in Denver to track down exactly who Russell Pace worked for. I got the number from her, then I called Amy. She had found nothing, no transmitter, no VCR unit. "You're sure you looked everywhere," I said.

"Everywhere in the back room. I didn't go into the saloon."

"And you're sure you know what you're looking for?"

"A little black rectangular box with a glass eye. It just wasn't there, Brew.

I didn't tell her about Dennis. The fewer people who knew about him now, the less stress for them. "I'll be back soon," I said.

"How soon?"

"A couple of days. Just go do your work. Forget about this until I get back."

After hanging up, I called Kate back and told her everything I knew.

"Sounds as though you've finally stumbled onto something for the AP," she said. "Any idea who they're protecting?"

"I don't even know which agency is doing the protecting. I saw an FBI ID, but that means nothing. I once was interviewed by a guy who flashed U.S. Postal Service Inspector ID who later turned out to be CIA. Sounds like CIA here, but I thought the Marshals were in charge of that Witness Protection Program."

"All the agencies work together on that, but you're right, it's the Marshal's office in Justice that does the actual transport and set-up. That's a pretty tough security thing to crack, if that's what you're after."

"I'm going to call that Mike Solo guy you keep talking about. If I can get the case re-opened with the evidence I think I'll have, there will be one fewer person in Kootenai Falls. Whoever it is will undoubtedly be re-relocated, if they are totally committed to keeping him a secret."

She sighed then and asked if I really thought there would be a security system tape.

"No one except the store owners, my cohort in Kootenai Falls and you and I know about the system, so once we let a few people know, there should be a lot of activity. But we have to find the damned thing first. It's there; I *know* it's there. Some goddamned place... tucked in where nobody could find it. That Gil Owen obviously had a special kind of genius for secrecy."

"I've got a great idea, Brew. I'll send an AP reporter up there to snoop around and ask questions. That'll get the juices flowing. I know somebody with great sources for a story like this one."

I said no, as it might be unhealthy for the poor unsuspecting AP guy. "But I am going to call that Solo fellow. Have you spoken to him lately?

"Not in a long while. He owes me a couple, including a major expensive dinner at La Cote´Basque."

"So — what do *you* think's going on here, Wells? Is this some big Mafia don in hiding or something? Like that guy who turned on Gotti? Seems like an odd place for a Sicilian thug to hideout."

"Could be anything," she said. "But the key is in that phrase about this guy being able to embarrass the government. There's a giveaway in that somewhere. Also, I don't think it'll embarrass the government, but it might nail the FBI or CIA to the wall in some way."

"Unless it's one of those Washington D.C. dealmakers... those campaign money runners."

"Or a former girlfriend of a former President. Brew, you'd better not go out without your bulletproof vest on if it's at all connected to the White House. It's very easy to neutralize, as they say. It only takes someone who's willing to do it. As easy here as it was for Stalin. All you need are a few frightened officials on the wrong side."

"Yeah," I said, "who's going to listen to complaints? Easiest way to get away with murder is to be the captain of the official investigating team."

"So be careful, dear one."

I told her I would. "Isn't it interesting — the murder at the Laughing Horse Inn is the key to unraveling all of this, and it isn't a murder at all. Well... maybe a *kind* of murder, since Dennis is cut off from his life, so to speak."

I hung up and went to the window and looked out at the yellow night — yellow because of the motel's parking lot lights. I wondered why I did not feel vulnerable. Perhaps because the year was heading toward mid-May. The May of even a troubled year still makes one feel invincible. Or maybe it was merely Jessie who helped dispel whatever jitters I should have been feeling.

Jess lay sleeping on her side again on her round bed on the floor between the two double beds. I wanted to kneel next to her and cup her head in my hands and tell her I loved her... but she was sleeping so soundly, snoring lightly.

"Michael Solo?" I asked.

"Who's this?"

"A friend of Kate Wells. She says you can sometimes help nailing down a government employee."

"It's late. Call me in the morning. Tell Wells to call me first." He hung up.

# Chapter Twenty-Five

Amy was at the paper when I pulled into Kootenai Falls late the next afternoon. Both man's and dog's spirits lifted and Jess sprang from one open window to the other, whimpering.

I stopped at a Conoco station and called Amy.

"Greta's okay. She's...."

"I know. Don't talk on the phone." I asked her to meet me out at my place.

I drove past my road a hundred yards to look at the Red Dog. There was yellow tape still in back, but the front was clear and open for business as usual. I drove back to my road, and when I pulled onto the property, Jessie immediately saw her sheep and began barking. "Not right away, old girl," I told her. "Got some unpacking to do first."

She raced through the door as I held it open for her, bounded to the top of the stairs and turned around and met me with a little fast dancing, her smile broad, her tongue flagging. She was exploding with delight at finally being back home. Later, when I let her out through the French doors, she ran down to the fence line and barked her hellos to the sheep and then to the llamas next door.

I called Solo; he'd talked with Kate and found out that Pace didn't work for the FBI. But that was all he could find out about him.

Amy looked good to me. She got out of her car and opened the trunk and took out a large manila envelope and a smaller white envelope and a small black box. The black box looked good to me, too.

She had on a white T-shirt and tight jeans and she looked very, very good to me. Too young of course, but nevertheless she looked good to me.

Very good.

# John Herrmann

What I'm trying to say is that she looked very, very good to me.

In less than ten minutes she looked even better, once she was out of the T-shirt and jeans.

It took some doing getting her out of those jeans.

"I'll never get them back on," she said.

"I may not let you ever put them back on," I told her. I kissed places I had forgotten she had, and I had forgotten how delicate she is and how responsive.

Don't get me wrong — I like responsive.

Responsive is good.


Later, with Jessie pretty much miffed at me, pouting, lying about and listless, not wanting to go out, Amy and I opened up the envelope. It held brochures picturing a magic clock — an electronics box with tiny camera and transmitter.

"Thanks to NASA, right?" I said. "I mean, miniaturization is the space program's gift to mankind."

"Forgive me for not showing a lot of excitement," she said. "I'm still a little glassy-eyed after.... You know?"

"I know," I said, turning the camera/transmitter box over in my hands. "You're the first woman I've slept with who gets me right away horny again five minutes later. There's just something about you. Maybe it's because you're rich."

"Yeah, rich makes me horny too. Except I'm not rich and neither are you."

"How do you know I'm not? Maybe this little camera will make us both rich."

"Because rich people don't live the way you live, and rich people don't screw the way you screw."

"You like the way I screw?"

I put down the clock as she leaned over and kissed my cheek. "Pretty much..., yeah. Pretty much I do." She spoke through her mussed hair, brushing at it absently, her eyes locked onto mine.

Jess sighed and lay flat out onto her side.

"I love you, too, Jessie," I said, but got no response. Not even an eyeball my way. She lay on her side staring at the wall.

There is no power on earth stronger than a jealous border collie.

"This lens," she said. "It's the size of a flea."

"Flip Phillips says it's wide angle."

"Who?"

"She runs the Satellite City store in Taos where they sell these. But anyway, what we really need is the other end." I showed her the photo on the back page of the brochure. "It's got to be there... somewhere. A video recorder and tape. It could be two-thousand feet from this transmitter, which means it could be a block away... in something like a truck or a building. It could also be anywhere if it's connected to satellite transmission."

"It could be in the back there, at Fred's butcher shop."

"Doubtful. Too much metal stuff there with all the cows hanging around on hooks, and the cooling equipment and locker. Too much interference. I'd expect Gil Owen to have it stuck where it would be very protected and out of the way. Not right in the computer office part. Where did you find the camera?"

"Above the outside door. It was facing inside the entrance to their office."

"Ouch! Too easy. How'd everybody miss it?"

"Sometimes you miss the obvious if you aren't careful. And no one knew about it anyway. There are dummy cameras in the bar part and the hallway, so that's probably as far as they looked."

"Anything else?" I asked.

"I've got that PI's report. You'll like it."

I asked what it said.

She opened the white envelope and pulled out a few sheets of paper. "This PI guy is amazing. He has contacts everywhere.

"Well, I have contacts as well," I said. "For instance, I got a desk clerk at the Best Western in Taos to go into its computer and find out for me that Able stayed there for three nights, May 4th, 5th and 6th. So — he's in on it," I said, mostly to myself.

"In on what?"

It was time, and so I told her. "Here's the shocker, Amy — Dennis is alive. I didn't want to tell you before. Burden and all that."

Her eyebrows raised, then she squinted and smiled. "No, nothing shocks me anymore about this. Unless it would be that you want your old job back."

I let that go. "How about this one: our friend from the FBI? The FBI never heard of him."

"Pace?"

"Russell Pace hisownself. You got it. The murder at the Laughing Horse Inn was an ushering of Dennis into the Witness Protection Program."

"But why does the FBI or whatever want to protect Dennis?"

"No," I said. "They're protecting themselves. It's some-one here in Kootenai Falls who is keeping something quiet about the federal government. If this thing were to blow wide open, this guy, whoever he is, would stand out like Jessie at a dog show."

I looked over the PI's report. "Nothing here about Peachart."

"He was around the whole time. So was Jim Letwilig."

"And Kellog?"

"In Sandpoint, getting his regular fix in armed insurrec-tion training. I told you."

I wondered about that Sandpoint location. Dennis had called me from Kramer, Idaho, and it's just north of there, just before he took off for Taos.

Amy went on: "The story going around about Kellog is that he's going to get together a few of his camo buddies and go down to Mexico to break his little brother out of jail."

"Lots of luck. There'll be two Letwiligs as guests of the Mexican government."

The report offered a few lines on the others — Leo and Alesandra and of course Greta were all where they said they were; there was information on who-where-when also on Howell (with information about the pending buy of the Red Dog), Toby Wales, Amy herself, Tom and Roxy and even about me. It finally showed nothing out of the ordinary and I didn't expect there would be, but I had to be certain.

Except one thing: nothing was out of the ordinary. And there always is something.

"You can't take a period of time in anyone's history and not have something seem strange or that some time element is un-accounted for. This is too pat."

Amy narrowed her eyes at me, possibly stifling a smirk. "You haven't lived in a small town long enough, Moore," she said. "Now what about you getting with Tom tomorrow. He says he wants you back."

"At half the salary and writing promotional pieces about Peri's Parenting Salon?"

"You could do worse. Peri has a wonderful thing going there for young parents."

"You're right," I said. "It's a good story. Interesting isn't it that we need instruction in parenting now. Not just a book like that Spock thing years ago."

I asked her if she thought the PI was thorough and she said yes, that he spent a lot of time on the locals.

I had an idea then and stood up. "Was Gil's repair truck

parked at the Dog when you went in to look for the VCR?"

"No. But it probably isn't Gil's. It is part of Leo's business," she said.

"So the truck *could* be at Stenopolis' house."

"You're right. And probably..."

"And probably... that's maybe where Gil stashed the receiver and recorder."


Alesandra Stenopolis was lying back deep in her chair draped in orange silk. She was spread out on the extra wide LazyBoy with a half-filled glass next to her right elbow and a half gallon jug of Jack Daniel's on the coffee table in front of her. And not surprising at all, Greta Hahn was still staying with her.

"I had those four rooms up on the third floor just going to waste," Stenopolis said.

"And this is the most friendly safe house in Yaak County," I said. "A good place for her. How's she doing?"

"A little disheveled. But one doesn't stay here-a-week, there-a-week without it wearing, does one?"

Amy and I sat down and explained again about the smallness of the camera and VCR and that there might be a tape of the crime. I asked to see the repair truck.

"There are two of them," she said, as Greta came into the room.

"I thought I heard your voice," Greta said.

"You're okay, are you?"

She dropped into a sofa and sighed. "I'd be a lot better if we could see an end to this." Her eyes were dark as though she had not been sleeping well. In all, she looked terrible. But there was a toughness about her that you could see through the forty-something sagginess. A determination maybe to survive whatever came along. You had to admire it. I thought it best not to burden her with the news of Dennis' resurrection or the chance that we'd find a taping of the Owens being killed. "Maybe just a few days more. And you'd best not leave here... for anything."

"So — what's going on?" she asked.

"Yes, dear boy, what *is* going on?" Stenopolis said.

"If you all know too much it might work against you," I said.

"And Amy," said Stenopolis. "It won't work against her? Just what is the danger now? And who are we being threatened by?"

"Amy Kroll can take care of herself," I said, smiling back at her and, of course, "seeing her" without her clothes on. (*Watch it, Brewster. This is going on too much. Yes, she looks good. Just keep your mind where it's supposed to be.*) Amy was taking in the unfamiliar scene — the strange ornate elegance of a room decorated by a heavy, ancient Greek broad with the taste of a carnival barker. "I'm just a bystander," she said to Stenopolis. "No one cares what a junior reporter thinks."

"And we here *cannot* take care of ourselves, is that it, Brewster?" Stenopolis said.

"Right now we're not sure just which side is after what. But what we're certain of is that government officials would like this to just go away. But Amy and I aren't going to let it."

"And you think Peachart or that FBI fellow would try to stop you?"

"Who knows. I've been warned, both in person and on the Internet. I doubt that there is any real federal policy to kill shit disturbers, but you never know. This Russell Pace, for instance. I once tried to check him out, and he didn't check out. The FBI didn't seem to know his name right away. It took a little while and then someone said, 'Oh *THAT* Russell Pace.' But by then it was clear to me that his FBI ID is a cover for something else. He's as much an FBI agent as I am."

"This is all very difficult for me to fathom," Stenopolis said. "This is a little town; things like this don't happen here."

"Why do you think I'm still in danger?" Greta asked.

"Because your boyfriend was working with the devil. You're now the closest living person to what he was working on. And someone might think you know too much and... well, you know the rest."

"But I don't *know* anything," she said, her hands flat against her temples. "He was helping Gil with some way to stop TV advertising."

"It doesn't matter what you know, or think you know," I said, reaching into my coat pocket for the disks. "These," I said, holding them up, "might as well be sticks of dynamite under government buildings."

Stenopolis leaned her hulking self forward. "What are they? They're not the anti-advertising things are they, Brew? Dennis told us that they somehow get... burned into the machine, is the way he put it."

Amy turned from the front window. "Yes, that's the first question, isn't it? That's what all this killing's been about."

I said to Stenopolis, "These three little disks I got from

your brother make anyone's Internet e-mail server into a security blanket. You normally send messages and servers always stamp your full name and e-mail return address on them. This little program removes the sender's identity before the server gets it and sends the message on to the addressee."

Greta eyes widened. "Where did you get those?" she whispered.

"So," Stenopolis said, "if you're planning to blow up the Oklahoma post office building, you can make your plans with your friends and not be traced."

"Exactly. Every other way of communicating can be traced or eavesdropped on. In-person, phone, fax, and formerly on the Net. There are ways of going through several servers on the Web, but they also, finally, are traceable now. But with this little gem of a program, you could make a thousand bombing plans you don't intend to carry out, and the federal government would have to take major precautions at all of the sites."

"The cost could be..."

"In the millions," I said. "It's not just a crank call or a phoned-in threat to bomb an airliner or anything. You could code them so that only the ones you intend would be known to your e-mail community. It would be the real thing — real plans. And to carry out one or two every so often would keep this country totally hostage. It would turn our society into a military playing field.

"Can you imagine the public reaction?" I said. "With this software, you could say you were going to bomb fifteen airliners in the next week, and no one could do anything about it except check every flight that left the ground every minute of every day for that week."

Stenopolis lay back, picking up her glass of JD on the way. "And it all began right here in Kootenai Falls at our little Red Dog Saloon. Who would have thought it?"

"And was probably sold to some nutty racist paramilitary-type group," I said. "These disks are just copies. The originals are out there, paid for in big bucks and three lives."

Amy said: "World War Two probably began in a pub, maybe on some meaningless Thursday night, with a short paperhanger who looked like Charlie Chaplin, a map of the world and a number two pencil. Fifteen years later, sixty-million people were dead."

"Well," I said, "this may not play out as all that significant. But there are plenty enough dead people here now. There is the question of justice, but also of humanity. I care about sixty-million dead people, and I care about Gil and Beth, Dennis and

Lynette, and I care about you too, Greta. Forget the ultimate outcome for now; look at those murders and you can get pretty damned sick at heart."

"But you never know," said Amy. "This could turn out to be as significant as anything that ever happened. You just never know."

# Chapter Twenty-Six

Leo Stenopolis is nearing eighty, a small man for a Greek, and an absolute slave. When Alesandra speaks, so much younger and so very capable of out-shouting anyone, Leo leaps. He is one of those small husbands who do everything around the house while the overstuffed woman spends his money on the telephone ordering planters and new draperies from upscale catalogues she receives because when she fills out those little purchase registration cards, she always checks the $150,000 - $300,000 family income category.

But — they are in the end a gentle couple well suited for one another, he having chosen her, she having endured an older man's shuffle for all of these years.

Leo took a ring of keys from his belt. "The one Gil used all the time is the Chevy van over there," he said, pointing. "I saw the system when it came in. It's about the size of a video tape. But I don't know where Gil put it. Might not of even gotten it up yet, for all I know. I left that kind of stuff up to him."

"Has anyone been in it since the cops let you drive it here?" I asked.

"To my knowledge no, it's been locked up since that Saturday night before Gil and Beth were shot."

We got it open and I looked inside. Except for seats and a few remnants of winter — a short-handled snow shovel, a bag of D-Icer — nothing more. An empty truck.

"I've got to get back into the store," I said to Leo. "The thing has got to either be there or somewhere around close by."


I will spare you the details of my search except to say that it took over an hour of going around a smallish room. I stopped first at the newspaper to talk with Tom, but he was out. I went down to the Kootenai Falls Cafe´ to find him, but found only the same cronies sipping coffee and commenting about a new tax. I sat at a table with the paper and had a bowl of chili and a mug of Earl Grey and read a nice story by Amy about Doc Pete leaving the lucrative world of a big city medical practice for "the promised land." Amy played up that Pete's talents were so far wasted because of the lack of current local high-tech diagnostic equipment. He spent a lot of time doing family practice.

In an hour I was at the back room of the Red Dog, fed, sleepy, and still thinking of Amy. How do you shake that? You don't. You live with the images and they become the good things tucked in around your life.

After an hour's search, I found the small brown case that must have held the units; it was on a high shelf at the back of the store. No one would have thought to look inside as it had the appearance of just another slick electronic toolbox.

It was unlocked... and empty of equipment. Inside, there were several more brochures pitching the different models available. I guessed that the whole thing — camera and transmitter, mini-VCR and receiving unit all had been neatly packed and shipped in the case. Also, a cardboard mockup of a TV satellite dish the size of my palm had been sitting on top of the case. I wondered if that meant that possibly Gil had gone for the expensive version.

But where was the recording unit with the tape? Working backward in time, it was clear that only three or four people knew of its existence: Gil and maybe Beth (and that's only an assumption), Leo and Dennis. And maybe Greta, but that's doubtful too.

But *after* the murders, how many more knew of it? Me, Amy, Alesandra, Leo. That's it.

Dennis is the only possibility of any of them who might have run off with the thing, but he's not around. He might have taken it before he left town. But that would just about add up to Dennis either being the killer or protecting the killer. Neither made sense, so I kept looking.

Teri and Ellen were working the bar and kitchen. While Ellen tossed together my usual shrimp cocktail, loaded with enough horseradish in the sauce to require a second or third mug of Moose Drool.

"I've always wanted to go down through there, and especially to Santa Fe."

"Santa Fe is a small version of Los Angeles now," I said.

"I heard you rattling around in back," she said. She poured herself a coke with shaky hands. It made me wonder: you overlook some good people when an awful crime is committed. I had overlooked Teri. Now, I studied her... her eyes, shaking hands.

"Something wrong?" I asked, hoping to catch her off guard.

"You're too damned perceptive for my own good," she said, smiling. "No — just worried about you... and all of this stuff." She took a sip of her coke.

"Here," I said, putting a five-dollar bill on the bar. "Sneak yourself a brandy or something." She grinned and pushed my ten back toward me and I shrugged.

My shrimp cocktail arrived then. Ellen held it out at arms length, her sweet smile meaning it was a six-alarm sauce mix.

"How many beers to cool me down after?"

She flashed her wide-eyed innocent look and said, straight-faced: "Just the way you like it, big boy."

The tiny black VCR box with the mini-tape was, as they say, hidden in plain sight. If you turn around on the stool at the center of the Red Dog bar and face the big screen TV, you see a Coor's Light neon sign. It lights up an area above the TV. After I had downed the mandatory small pitcher of Moose Drool, I turned to see what the weather would be tomorrow in Seattle — and I saw a metal box that looked as if it belonged to the TV... with an aerial of some sort. I turned back and was about to say something to Teri about the expected warming trend when it hit me.

I walked up to the screen, dragged a chair over and stood on it. And there it was.

When I got back to Stenopolis's place, the black box hidden in the Pathfinder's arm rest well, Bob Able was standing at the front window.

"We have to talk," he said turning toward me.

"Not hello, go to hell or anything, right, Bob?"

"Did you call the AP with that story?"

"What story is that?"

"Two of the Washington papers and *The Missoulian* had a story by the AP connecting the killings here with the federal Witness Protection Program. Where would they get that except from you?"

"Well, here's a question for *you*, Bob? How was Taos?"

If you would not have been looking as closely as I, you might have missed that slightest of flutter in his eyes at my mention of Taos. Seemingly without dropping a beat, he said again, "You brought in the AP and all of this publicity we don't need around here. Besides, it is a wholly inaccurate story. Totally made up."

"I have no power to bring in anybody, Bob. I helped a friend file a story about what's been going on in Kootenai Falls, if that's what you mean. It's my profession... filing stories."

"The case is closed, Moore. The homicides were committed by someone who has himself been murdered. There is no need to push this further. Case closed."

"I see. But obviously some lone AP editor out there sees it differently."

"Because of your constant interference."

"Now boys," Stenopolis said, "why don't you come over here. Sit. *Sit!* Have tea with me." Tea indeed.

Amy sat silent in a deep overstuffed chair in a dark corner of the room. I couldn't see her face but I knew she was smiling.

Strange, the things that run though one's mind at the most inappropriate moments. With Able in front of me shaking with rage, I imagined Amy's small breasts, and her whiteness, as she lay on her back on my sheets and, as I approach her, growling like a small northern Minnesota fur-bearing animal.

Obviously she was smiling over there in the dark, having just read my mind.

To Amy I said, "I found what I was looking for, by the way." She nodded. Able looked at me with flashing eyes. "So," I said to Able, "what were you doing in Taos? Anything to do with the Witness Protection Program?"

He scowled at me. "If the newswire puts any more of this out, we're going to have major problems around here."

"No — *you're* going to have major problems."

"The community, I mean."

"Well, I've got an attention getter, Bob. It seems there was video surveillance equipment that Gil installed to watch over his shop. Apparently he felt the projects were important enough to spend a bunch of money on protecting them."

"Is there a tape?"

"Yes, there is."

"Have you seen it?" He was not as frantic as I'd hoped for.

"Not yet."

"And?"

"It could have the murder scene on it, yes."

He sighed deeply and said to Stenopolis: "It doesn't register with this guy." To me he said: "You're way over your head,

Moore. You're messing around in something you have no business in. This is a small town. This is a very, very small town, my friend." He did what he could with body language to appear menacing: narrowed, squinty eyes and as pinched a face as a cool, small town attorney can manage. "Everyone knows everything that happens here. You let this get out to the wires, I'm telling you, there will be hell to pay."

I shook him off. "Getting back to the subject here, Bob," I said, dismissing his anger, "what exactly were you doing in Taos? We had you tracked down, so don't bother denying it."

He dropped his arms to his sides and raised his eyes to the ceiling. "Nothing I've said has gotten through to him."

"Brew, sit down for a minute," Stenopolis said. "Let the man tell his story."

"We have him in Taos, and it looks like Bob here arranged for Dennis O'Brien to appear to be dead, killed, strangled. Yes, I said *appeared*."

I had their attention then. You could have cut the angst in the air with a banana.

"Truth is, Dennis is alive and well and himself drafted into the so-called Protection Program, isn't he, Bob?"

"Dennis not... *dead?*" Stenopolis said to herself. Then, after a truly handsome swig of JD, she added, "I don't know whether to jump up for joy or weep in despair. Why on earth would they take Dennis away like that?"

"What's bothering Bob here is what has been going on here in Kootenai Falls for a very long time now. Isn't that what's bothering you, Counselor?"

"So you *did* talk to the AP," Able said. He was silent then, red-faced and furious.

I went on: "Helpful Bob here is a kind of conduit for the U.S. Marshal's office. He helped Dennis get out of Dodge, so to speak, and got him safely to home base. Seems as though Dennis was a Taos Pueblo Indian, descendants of the extinct Anasazis, some say. But that history is unclear. Anyway, Dennis is originally from the Taos Pueblo. He's not Hopi. Which, by the way, throws a big wrench into that Hopi-eagle feathers theory that pointed to Dennis as the killer, as that is a Hopi tradition and has nothing at all to do with Indians of the Pueblo. Eagle feathers are used by Hopis in certain religious ceremonies, but not by Pueblo Indians. Our real murderer didn't know that Dennis was from Taos.

"Whoever the killer is, he was convinced that Dennis was Hopi. And he was very, very wrong. But Bob here gets Dennis to Taos where Dennis feels safe. Then the feds go to work and talk

Dennis into changing his identity. And Dennis has nothing to lose but his ass here in Kootenai Falls, as he would surely be extradited. So Dennis agrees and rides off into the anonymity of the government's program. For what reason? You want to tell us, Counselor?"

All the air was out of Bob Able's body.

"No? All right, then I'll do it. The reason that Dennis O'Brien wasn't brought back here to stand trial is because it would have revealed that there is someone here in Kootenai Falls living a new life under that same Witness Protection Program. And what is more likely — that someone, admits the government, was *involved* with the militia goings here. He's no doubt either the purchaser of the original software, or an agent for them. It is also possible that this person was either the killer of the Owens and Okla, or the arranger, or at least a part of the motivation for their execution.

"And why wasn't Dennis simply murdered?" I said, pausing for dramatic effect: "The way I see it — Dennis wasn't murdered in Taos *or* here because it was necessary to have a scapegoat... someone to take the heat. Otherwise, the investigation could get sticky. And it just wasn't necessary to have him killed if he'd cooperate. And of course he did exactly that. It was much more to the point to relocate Dennis than to kill him.

"Bottom line here: our government would rather see a murderer go unpunished than suffer a major embarrassment."

"None of this has to happen," Able said. "We can talk about it and stop it right here. We don't have to go on with this."

"Oh *don't* we?" I said, perhaps too loudly. Amy stood up. Greta came into the room. I wondered how much she'd heard; if she knew her former boyfriend was still alive.

Greta's hands were shaking.

Stenopolis took another sip of her drink. The bottle looked very inviting to me, but I was in need of staying clear-headed and made the supreme sacrifice.

Able spun around and stared at Greta. "Did you know — about Dennis?"

She had a hard time saying it but nodded that she'd overheard us. Her hands and shoulders were shaking.

"I say we call in Peachart and Toby Wales right about now. What do you say, Counselor? Are you game? We could sit right down here and watch our movie."

He sat across from Stenopolis, his hands fixed on his knees. "Y'all don't understand." He was looking at Stenopolis in a pleading way, leaning forward, pressing his hands down hard. "There is a lot of pressure."

"On whom?" Stenopolis asked.

"I'm sworn to secrecy here," he said. "They'd have my license if I told you."

"Does Peachart know?" I asked.

"I can't speak for anyone else," he said.

"But you assume he does."

Greta backed off, her hands trembling. Poor gal, I thought. To have been the object of an execution-style murder once removed was beating her down. Anyone could see that.

"He's alive, Greta," I said. "Dennis is alive. If you never see him again, at least you know that he's safe."

She turned away, her hand to her mouth, and left the room.

I know shock registers differently with different people. But she reacted as though I'd said Dennis was dead rather than alive.

Maybe after a while shock is shock. The theory of a straw and a camel's back.

I might not have done as well as she, had one of my friends been shot dead because he was mistaken for me. That can wrap you pretty tight.

"Able, whether you or the feds or anyone else likes it or not, this thing is going to be re-opened. I'm sure the tape will show us why it should be. Which means that the government is going to have to come in and do whatever it needs to do in the open."

"Look," Able said, "you have here a secret the government wants kept, and the stakes are high. Higher than you could ever imagine. Then you have Vreeland who wants to be governor. You have absolutely no evidence that Dennis O'Brien wasn't murdered, at least none that will stick. And you have Dennis' killer in a Taos jail. You tell *me* how this is going to bust wide open."

He had a point. But I knew what I knew, and that was enough for me.

"The doctor in Taos who signed the death certificate confessed to me she hadn't seen a body. And last but certainly not least — and something you didn't count on — is the fact that there is a high-tech surveillance camera and tape of the killings up there at the Red Dog."

Able shook his head. "If there is this tape you talk about — and I seriously doubt that there is, since none of our investigators came up with anything like it — it wouldn't make it to the hearing. You're forgetting that there isn't anyone in any official capacity ready to stick his neck out to re-open the case."

He spoke the truth, of course: "You could have ten tapes and the murderer screaming his guilt all over the place — but it wouldn't come to trial. That's because nobody *wants* it to come to trial, Moore. Nobody who matters."

He stood up and walked over to the front window. A funny little dandy, always in a suit and tie. You wonder how these guys get this way.

"You're very naive, Brew," he continued. "For a man who has lived the life you have, you seem to have missed a big part of what makes our society tick. There are two things butting heads here: number one: the system of justice, where we try to right wrongs. And number two: the overall *balance* of justice, and that's where we try to maintain what little semblance of civilized society we have. It's not often that these two come into a collision course, but when they do, number one takes a back seat. The larger concern wins out every time, that of protecting the culture. And maybe that might just be at the expense of a moment here and a moment there of injustice."

"That's a specious argument," Amy said. "Justice means looking for the truth as often as you can, and when you find it, making it public. It's so simple, Bob, that most of you lawyers miss it. That's a cliché, but it's true."

"Wouldn't it be swell if things worked that way," he said, his hands out as though showing the size of a trout.

"Bullshit, Bob." Amy turned her back to him.

"So, I'll ask it again," I said, "let's make that call to the sheriff's office and get the ball rolling."

"I think," Stenopolis said, slowly, "I *really* think, Bob, government is foolish to try to put a lid on. In the *long* run, I mean." She was now leaning forward for emphasis on "long."

It was getting late and when I tried to get Peachart by phone, I got an answering machine. I left a message to call me immediately, but I knew better. But I'd nail him first thing the next morning.

# Chapter Twenty-Seven

It was late but I could not have slept without looking at the surveillance tape. The mini-tape fit into a slot in a standard VCR dummy. I shoved it into my VCR and Amy and I settled down for the show.

It was a motion sensitive system so that there was no waste unless someone or thing came into the camera's field of vision. The images were dated and they began on the day before the murders, Friday April 24th. Time of day was also flashed to the right side of the date.

The first static still was of Gil. The series of stills showed him moving into the back office. He was out of sight after a half dozen frames.

"The camera must have been placed just to show the entrance to the office," I said.

"You'd think he'd have aimed it at his computer equipment," Amy said.

"Too much movement. The camera had to be placed where it would catch whoever went in or out but not the constant movement of a working situation."

There were three more "sessions" of stills, all marked with date and time. On the series dated April 25, 10:12 P.M., you view the back of Beth going into the office from the Red Dog area. Again, about six stills and then nothing.

Then came the series we had hoped would be there.

It was dated 11:23 P.M. the same night and was a shot of of Beth's back once again. She is backing away out of the office. After four stills, there is included in the upper right another figure... someone wearing a raincoat and wide-brimmed hat pulled down. It is one of those old-fashioned felt hats one would see on Alan Ladd or Dana Andrews in some *film noire*. The person's face is not visible, but he is slightly taller than Beth. Weight however is disguised by the coat.

Beth appears to be turning, perhaps to run, one leg out to the side and an arm in mid-swing. But then in the next still she falters, one more shows her head suddenly arched forward, and the next stills are of her crumbling to the floor and out of the camera's view but no doubt exactly where I had seen her body the next day.

The killer shows up then in a full frontal image. But again, the Alan Ladd hat is pulled down too far to see the killer's face. That along with the large trench coat is the perfect disguise. If he were to rob a bank, there would be no telling details on film.

The next series is of only a portion of hat, a raised arm, and both Amy and I knew what was going on out of view of the lens. Then, suddenly, the killer is standing once again, facing the camera. You see a series showing the pistol push out in front of him, one in which there is smoke rising from the killer's outstretched arm. You also see that he is wearing at least one glove. You also know that what has been captured is Gil showing up at the hallway and being shot.

The hat fills the scene next, then there is a short series of the back of the killer moving in toward the office. Then nothing more of the murder scene. The next stills are of Toby Wales and other uniformed police, and I turned off the TV and VCR then.

"He must have left by the back door," Amy said.

I said nothing. It was too eerie a feeling seeing someone you knew well die in a made-for-TV docu-drama. It was not easy speaking then, but I managed to say that we had to protect the tape.

"It doesn't show enough of the killer to do any good," Amy said.

"Yes it does," I said. "If the killer isn't Dennis, I know who it is. And it isn't Leo. Leo is shorter by far, and stooped."

"Then — Dennis?" she said.

"Maybe."

I called Kate who said what I expected — that it would not be easy getting anything from Justice on the relocation program. "Call Mike Solo again," she said.

"What's his story anyway?" I asked.

"He was with Justice forever until a few Christmases ago. He gave himself a big present — he quit. Say... what time is it, anyway?"

"Late. I'm sorry, Kate, but this is important. Is Solo really a good source? I've only talked to him that once and it was a simple ID."

I imagined Kate's smile. "Do I ever give you anything other than good?"

"No," I said. "Kate always gives good good." I told her we had the tape and what was on it.

"Not much to go on then, is it?"

"Enough, maybe. It shows the killer anyway, and his clothing. That's something."

After I hummed a few bars of "As Time Goes By" and Kate slurped me a kiss from 3,000 miles away, I hung up and dialed and got Solo right away, as though he had been sitting on the phone. "How is Kate?" Solo asked, his voice brittle.

"She says you're supposed to be taking her to Tavern on the Green, or else you're in big trouble."

"Tell her I'll be there soon. So — what are you looking for this time?"

"Whatever you can find out about the Witness Protection Program in northwest Montana?"

He chuckled. "You can't call somebody and ask who the folks are in your area who don't want to be found. That's the whole purpose of the Program."

I told him about the murders, the set-up of Dennis, the phony murder in Taos, and then about the guy in the park who warned me to cool it.

"Stinks to high heaven, doesn't it?" Solo said. "It always does. That's the dirtiest little segment of Justice, which is pretty damned dirty all over."

"What fries me is they avoid embarrassment at the expense of nailing a killer, and they send an innocent Indian kid into hiding."

"I'll make a couple of calls tomorrow. It's too late now. You might try hacking a little. Their computer security is about as good as their organizational skills. And you know what that means."

"I'm no hacker."

"Rent a hacker... by the hour. Someone you can trust."

Immediately Jim Letwilig came to mind, along with a quick negative. I wasn't going to involve him in this. He had enough troubles. He also wasn't totally off my list of possibles. Except that I felt in my gut that Jim wouldn't hurt a mosquito. Anyone who could brawl with his brother and never land or receive a punch had to view life and the militia with a sense of humor.

Solo gave me two Web sites to start with. "One's just the Justice Department's home page. But it's a consumer gateway and gives names and e-mail addresses. The other — well, you just try it and see what you get."

"And the calls you're going to make?"

"I'll get back to you when I have something," he said.

I asked Amy to work with me on the computer in the morning. We went to bed then, both of us wrapped in a gathered parachute of heaviness. I played and replayed in my drifting mind the images of Beth turning, leg and arm swinging, being threatened, being shot. Strange, but the image always came to me in color, though the video was in black and white.

Before I let myself go down into the mouth of sleep I remembered years ago seeing "The Misfits" when both Clark Gable and Marilyn Monroe were dead. It was for me the first film in which I saw dead actors talking to one another. I felt chilled by it then. But now, years later, after many of the great film actors and actresses have died but live up there on the big screen,... somehow now it's less chilling. I've gotten used to it. Death is less a shock for me now.

Sleep came finally, Amy against my side, her foot over my leg.

It was just after 7:00 A.M. when we logged onto the Net and tried the first "address," copied down names and information. Then I tried the second. It splashed lines of code onto my screen at first, then blipped a couple of times and asked for my user name and password. I knew it was useless to use any of the names I had so I just put in RUSSELL PACE for a user name and SLC (Salt Lake City) for a password.

No luck.

I tried Pace again with CIA for a password.

Still no luck.

"Here," Amy said. "Try this." She just tapped in his name twice and — what do you know! The thing opened like a flower.

"That's an old trick," she said. "People will use their name twice because it's easy to remember. My guess is that the Web address itself is the department's first line of security. No one except Justice agents had it, so the need for security beyond keeping the address secret isn't a concern."

I was into the system now, but into what? All I had was a blinking cursor. Nothing to tell me what to go for. A blank screen and a blinking cursor.

Amy moved behind me. "What are you going to do?" she asked.

"I don't know. Maybe nothing. Tinker," I said. "Will you make me a cup of Earl Grey?"

"My pleasure, sir," she said and kissed the back of my head.

I typed KOOTENAI FALLS, pressed return and got "Unknown Agent."

"OK," Amy said. "You're at an agent file gateway."

I typed in Pace's name again and code again began rolling down my screen. I highlighted the first line and got a file on a "Daniel K.D." It listed age, number of dependents, amount of monthly stipend, his new Social Security number, state of health, date of agreement to enter the protective system, and "Location #17033-717/."

"That's a ZIP and an Area Code," Solo said. "It could be where they took him in or it could be where he is now. It could also be a coded misdirection. Say the guy comes into the Program from New York and goes to Idaho. You put in central Pennsylvania ZIP and Area codes that stand for, say 94043-415, which is Mountain View, California. Not much help either though without a last name. In his former life he was probably neither Daniel nor a K.D. That's all code. Anyway," he said, "I called Kate."

"Checking me out?"

"I think I can help you. But you're going to have a problem on your hands if you..."

"They already know I'm on to them."

"They can be dangerous," he said.

"They already have been," I said.

"Well — here goes. There are several in the Program in the Yaak County area."

"I'd heard there was."

"Mostly drug informants, some from the L.A. gangs. One from southern Arkansas. And there is one guy from an L.A. gang who lived in Frisco and was high up in regular drug running. There is another, a woman, who knew too much about an Iranian couple who were brought over here by the CIA when the Shah got run out of his country. I saw the set up. Very slick. The Iranians were given phony doctorates from an obscure university and the agency got them teaching jobs in South Dakota. Obviously no one ever bothers to check the legitimacy of degrees on a resume´ these days.

"Mostly these are young people, compared with the old days when it was mostly Sicilians," he said. "But think about it: who would you want this guy in Kootenai Falls to be, if you could pick someone out?"

I hardly needed to hesitate on that one. "The Indian's attorney. He's a real jerk, one of the wealthy racists in our midst."

"That's one you can rule out. If you want them to be it, they never are. You can also sometimes rule out anyone who is high profile. But not always."

I said: "This guy's one of the group trying to keep the murder case closed. That's after trying to railroad the Indian. I can tell you that the case against Dennis O'Brien will not be reopened without exposing the government's motive for wanting it to go away. Not even with a video tape of the crime, which we have."

"You have a tape?"

"It shows the killer but not his face."

"Too bad. But maybe with some work you can figure it out."

"I may have figured it out anyway," I said trying to sound hopeful.

"The way I read it, your Indian wouldn't make it back into Kootenai Falls alive if you *did* find him," Solo said.

"That's so hard for me to believe about this government. But I guess I have to. Anyway, I'm not looking for the Indian, I'm looking for someone very embarrassing to our system of justice."

"It's not the government, Brew, it's a couple of idiots acting for the government."

I told him about the untraceable e-mail address program.

"There are other ways of doing that," he said.

"My understanding is that all of them involve going through a couple of servers to wash out the original ID and address and replace it every time it goes through another server. It's still traceable. A clever operator could track it down with persistence. But not with this Owen program. It's apparently flawless."

"You could follow the money. Someone got top dollar for that little piece of magic." Solo breathed out a sigh. "Anyway, I am going to talk to a couple of old friends and will be calling you back shortly. I just wanted you to know that I'd called Kate and that I'll work on it."

"How shortly?"

"As soon as I have something."

It was coming together for me. Clearly, before Gil and Beth were killed there were very few people who knew about the surveillance system. That fact began ringing in my ears. Maybe I'd get lucky and see the guy on the street wearing the raincoat. It is, after all, a small town. I had to chuckle at the idea of that kind of slip. But in reality, the very fact of wearing a disguise was important.

Amy said, "With Gil and Beth dead and Dennis out of the picture, I think the killer still thinks the sale of the software is a safe secret."

"Which means the buyer might want to target him. A secret is only as safe as the numbers of people who don't know about it. So far, public information reads this way: except for you and me and Dennis, everyone who knew about the disks outside of the buying group is dead. Unless there was a middleman seller. I was told by the FBI guy in Taos that they knew who the original buyer is."

Amy seemed to hold her breath. "It's the same person as the guy they stashed in the witness program..."

"...or how would the feds know. You're right!"

The phone rang then. It was Stenopolis.

"Someone just shot at Greta," she said. She said Greta had started over to her own house, perhaps hoping the early hour would allow her to get in, get some things, and get back to Stenopolis' house without being seen.

"Is she all right?" I asked.

"She's falling apart, Brewster. What do you expect of the poor girl? And I don't like all of this shooting around here. I'm going to call the police."

"I'd be surprised if one of your neighbors hasn't done that already."

# Chapter Twenty-Eight

I got to the bridge over the Elk River in twelve minutes and you could see an aura of blue and white lights flashing in the southeast part of town. When I pulled up at Stenopolis' house there were patrol cars everywhere, parked on the lawn, parked sideways on the street.

Two gray sedans were parked across the street, each with an almost invisible wire antenna sticking up from the right back fender. The FBI had suddenly made themselves visible.

When I entered the house, Stenopolis' hands were shaking. She was standing in the middle of the room, Greta behind her, talking with Russell Pace and another official-looking federal agent in a gray pinstriped suit. Detective Wales was standing at the front window looking out, and there were two more uniformed sheriff's deputies posted at the front door — Harry Bedford, who looked as though he had another year to go in high school, and Fred somebody, a recent hire I hadn't met.

Kootenai Falls had just scraped together enough public funds to field its own city police department, and most of us found we didn't know the cops well yet.

"Brew," Stenopolis said. It was an appeal more than greeting.

"What's going on?" I asked.

"Hello again, Mr. Moore," Pace said.

"Someone tried to shoot Greta!" Stenopolis said, as if I hadn't truly heard her on the phone. Her eyebrows were raised as though asking *me* to explain. "It's still going on, Brew." She touched two fingers to her lips to stop her hand from shaking.

Leo walked into the room from the back door and said, "Shot up my Nissan pickup. Windshield's gone. A shot went through the radiator into the goddamned block." His arms were outstretched showing the bigness of the damage.

I asked Greta if she was all right.

She nodded silently as Pace interrupted: "We'll be right with you, Mr. Moore. Have a seat. We'll need to talk to you as well."

# MURDER AT THE RED DOG

It was overwarm in the room, but something other than central heat made me uncomfortable. I took off my jacket and pulled at my sweatshirt collar. Greta apparently had not gotten out of the driveway and onto the street before the shots turned her back to the house.

I moved over to Toby at the window. "Do they know yet who was after Greta?" I asked, not expecting much from him. But Toby and I had always gotten on well, so I wasn't shy about asking.

"I can't say anything right now, Brew," he said. "But it's a damned mess."

"Where's Peachart? You'd think he'd want to be right in the middle." I half expected Toby to say it was Peachart who'd gone after Greta. He didn't.

"He's a cool one, that Vreeland is," Toby said. "He ducked out of town when the FBI rolled in this morning. Too much chaos for a man trying to get to the governor's office, I guess. He called in a while ago saying he'd be around if he was *really* needed."

The hand-held radio in Pace's pocket squawked and his hand grabbed for it. "We have Baron and we're rolling," said the crackling voice. Pace spoke into the unit: "Just do it. Then, suddenly, Toby turned away from the window and looked at Pace. "You... sonofabitch," he said, under his breath. He darted for the front door, but Pace was right after him. Toby made the door first, turned and pointed at Pace.

"Just stay where you are. This is *my* jurisdiction!" Then he turned back toward the door.

"I'm in charge here," Pace said. "This is federal government business." But Wales was already out of the door, running for his squad car. Pace looked back at his partner. "Tell Gerry to go get Wales."

The other agent nodded and picked his radio out of a holster on his belt and called outside, presumably to one of the gray sedans.

"What's going on?" I said. I looked at Greta who was backing toward a chair. Her body sagged and the lines of her face were deep, her eyes dark. She looked like a woman beyond feeling.

No response from Pace, so I pushed: "Wait for the PR spin, is that it? I've got a pretty good handle on it so far anyway, but I thought you might clear up a few things... like why the government continues to protect someone who continues to commit crimes."

Pace turned away. Speaking to Stenopolis, he said, "We'll

151

get Greta help with moving back into her own place."

Greta sat in a straight-back chair shaking her head no. I wasn't clear if it was *no, I don't want to go home*, or *I want this all to go away.*

The uniformed cops also had their portable radios, and both crackled and then Toby Wales' voice came over the scratchy speakers: "Harry, relay to MHP I'm westbound on Highway Two in pursuit of a gray Dodge with Utah plates. Let me know if anyone is heading east from Troy to intercept."

"Ten four," Harry said. "This is 861, dispatcher. Did you get that?"

"861, we got that. We'll relaying MHP."

"That's enough of that," Pace shouted.

Harry looked at him, then motioned for his partner to handle Pace. "Dispatcher: Detective Wales asks for backup. He's in pursuit of a gray sedan with Utah plates. They'd just about be at the west edge of town by now on Highway Two."

"So you're *re*-relocating your man right under our noses," I said. "What's his code name now... Baron? As in 'Red Baron?'"

He stopped and nailed me with his eyes. "That's enough. I want you outside of this house."

"Oh, no no no no," said Alesandra Stenopolis. She stood slowly and, as it were, occupied, or took possession of, the room. "I want him *inside* of this house," she said pointing at the deputy. "*Ins*ide of this house. This is *my* house. It doesn't belong to the FBI. You are guests here — for the time being."

Pace fixed a stare at Stenopolis but said nothing.

"I have no intention of interfering, Mr. Pace," she said. "Neither do my friends here. But this is private property you're on." She took a deep breath and then said, "They have my permission to cooperate completely with you. I want them to stay here and help in any way they can." The last of it trailed off in a way that is both soft and sinister.

Pace turned away, shaking his head.

The police radios squawked again. "Harry, this is Wales. There's been a landslide out here and I need a tow truck. We've got them stopped at mile marker thirty; part of their car is buried in mud. I'm arresting Hiram Howell on three counts of suspicion of murder and one count of assault with intent to commit murder. Tell the dispatcher to get the paperwork started."

Greta put her head down in her hands. Her back shook with her sobbing.

The dispatcher broke in then and acknowledged the request saying it would be ready when Wales got back to town.

"I'm also arresting agents Robert Harvey and Gerald Morgan of the FBI. Find out what the most serious charge is for interfering with a police action and giving false information to an officer."

Pace took out his own radio then. "Gerry, this is Pace."

No reply. No reply to two more attempts.

"Keller?" Pace said into his radio.

"I heard," came the response. "I'm out front."

Pace pointed at Officer Harry Bedford as if his finger alone could stop him. To his credit, Bedford simply strolled out of the room.

"I have copies of that software program, Pace," I said. But he wasn't interested in software. He couldn't care less about the implications of untraceable terrorist messages. That would be a project for the *real* FBI. As he turned to leave, I called after him: "Going back to Langley, Pace?" He stopped walking for an instant, his back to me, then walked toward where his flunky Keller was standing, holding the door open for his master.

You watch a man like Russell Pace walk away and you see his legs move, his arms swing as he walks. A man like Pace isn't paid to lose and he isn't used to losing and you can see it in how his arms swing, and his walk shows you the seriousness of losing. When a man like Pace gets into his gray government car, and its window flashes silver as the door closes, you know you will never see him again. And that is the best part of knowing such a man as Russell Pace.

# Chapter Twenty-Nine

There was little more to do that night except get in the way of the various bookings. Jessie was less than thrilled with the length of time that she'd spent alone, but she could not hide her forgiveness.

She met me at the cabin door with her great smile, her tail making circles behind. "I've got work to do, sweet girl. We ID-ed the relocation guy, now to dig up his history and what he has on the CIA."

Jessie circled once then flopped down next to the computer, and I went to work. "I've got a golden source, babe, so let's get on it."

It was just after noon when I phoned Amy. "I have some exciting news for you."

"I've been hearing all the excitement on the scanner. It's been keeping me awake here at my desk."

"Well, right now the police think Howell is the killer." I said. "Not that Pace and that bunch really care, except to cover it up."

"And you don't?"

"I think I know who the killer is. I just don't know the *why* of the killing yet. But Howell — he made that phone offer to buy the Red Dog, and you know why?"

"Jesus Christ, Brew, let me in on it."

"By then he knew about the camera and tape. Making an offer to buy gave him *carte blanche* to roam around the place and look for it."

"So," she said, "is he the murderer?"

"Not sure yet, pal. But I have a good idea of who it is. If I told you, you'd run down and write the story today."

"Of course!"

"So — in the morning, my love. In the morning, or whenever I get my stuff put together."

"I hate you," she said.

"I know," I said. "I'm so terribly fascinating. It's awful. Depressing. Depressing for someone with my intelligence and good looks to be so...." But she had hung up before I could finish.

I called Solo, got his answering machine. "See what you can find out about Hiram Howell," I said.

# Chapter Thirty

The next morning was May 20th. Nearly a month had passed since Gil and Beth and Lynette had been killed. They all had been laid into their graves, Lynette's body having been transported back somewhere in the Midwest where she still had family. Following the burials, and the long days after of murmuring about the sadness the families went through, we edged into warmer spring air. Much of the snow on the peaks around Kootenai Falls had thinned. Each morning the sun blazed through my bedroom window, and on May 20th, as I lay sleeping late for a change, the phone rang and it was Michael Solo.

"You'll never guess," he said.

"He's Mafia."

"Worse. He's not even a U.S. citizen." He said he'd sent an e-mail file to me a few minutes before. "We got lucky. Too many people in too many agencies know about this guy. If you want to keep a secret, my friend, don't tell it to the CIA. That's like taking out an ad."

I asked how he got what he got.

"There was all of this approval stuff for him to get licenses. Then there was Social Security. That's the easy one to crack. It's also going to be interesting to see how they explain a noncitizen getting Social Security and Medicare benefits for over thirteen years."

"You're a genius, Michael. Are you *my* source now?"

"When you're down this way, stop by. There are a couple of good people I'd like you to meet. Also, there are a few good micro-breweries worth our time."

"Done deal," I told him.

"We have some good stories to tell, if you're trustworthy."

"Ask Kate. I've never burned a source yet."

"We'll see about that," he said.

I printed out Solo's message. It came out of the printer

like a thing of beauty, three sheets delicately piled atop one another.

I showered, dressed, called Kate and thanked her answering machine, then called Amy and told her to meet me at the library. I told Jessie that she had to watch her sheep for me today, which seemed okay with her. She ran out to the fence line, barked a few times then looked back at me, her tail up. "I'm ready, boss," she was saying as hard as she could with her body.

I couldn't let her down. I went over, opened the gate and said "come bye." She raced out about fifty yards in a wide circle to the left, came around the sheep to the top of the balance point and then stopped. "Walk up," I yelled, and she did that.


Howell spent the night in the county lockup, but the two FBI agents had been booked and then released after a call had come through from Utah saying they would not pursue their activities and that they were informing the U.S. Marshal in charge of western Montana that Hiram Howell was no longer in the Witness Protection Program.

"Howell came here from Germany a couple of years after World War Two," I told Amy. "He had lived in East Germany, in a town near the Polish border."

We sat at a round table in the library in the same building as the Yaak County Court House.

"Where'd you get this?"

"Sorry," I said. "Best you don't know for now. It's called..."

"I know, burning your sources. But how does one go about getting sources to crack the U.S. Marshal's files?"

"If I die, you can have my Kate Wells for a source. But no sooner," I said. "Anyway, Howell's real name is Gerhardt Gurster."

"And...?"

"Here's your story... unless Tom won't print it."

"I'll find a home for it," she said, her hands flat on the table before her.

"Howell somehow got through the Wall to the West and went from Berlin to the U.S. Air Force intelligence base in Wiesbaden with what he knew about the communist spy apparatus. It was enough to get him a free ride to the States and a new identity."

"Why the new identity?" she asked.

"Because he was a Nazi camp guard. He is charged by the Israelis with marching thousands of people to the gas chambers in Poland. The Simon Wiesenthal people have him on their shit list as well.

"So — here is the U.S. government, the CIA, getting handed by Gurster some probably redundant information and rewarding a twenty-eight-year-old Nazi war criminal with lifelong perks."

"And he ends up in Montana?" Amy said.

"Only after several moves," I said. "Howell-Gurster had been married to a German woman who also was spirited out of East Germany to join him in Upstate New York." I looked at Solo's message. "They lived in Onteago, New York, until their first child was born, in 1953. Then there was some trouble about the paperwork. Apparently, living that close to Canada makes hospitals more careful about their record keeping. My source says they were moved by the marshals without the birth certificate being 'fixed' by the agency. I called about that and it's true. The child was not listed on any records in the city or county there.

"They were moved to Tucson because Willa Howell had developed a bronchial condition. They had one more child in 1956, a boy who received the proper live birth certificate but who died a few hours after being born.

"But the bronchial condition wasn't the real reason for the relocation," I said. "Seems that our friend was continuing to be a good Nazi. He had participated in a few white supremacist functions up there in Onteago and Port Deerfield."

"Nice for the CIA," she said. "Nothing like hiding an embarrassment with a big mouth."

"Exactly. Their worst fears realized. Then the next move was here, in 1973. Just the two of them — Willa and Gerhardt, who was firmly fixed on records everywhere as Hiram Howell. Willa died sometime later, I haven't got a date or cause of death."

"And the surviving child?"

"Nothing after the two of them were moved to Kootenai Falls. Apparently she moved out after high school. Maybe to go to college. There are no records my source could find about her after that."

"And before that?"

"I found out myself. I'm getting pretty nimble on that old Internet thing. Anyway, it appears that she had been enrolled in the Tucson school district."

"A she?"

"Yes. A daughter. Are you ahead of me? She was enrolled in the fall of 1959 in the first grade at Ocotillo Elementary School in Tucson as Greta Howell."

"So part of our story here," I said, "becomes one of an unreconstructed Nazi war criminal and lifelong white supremacist buying up software for his pals' protection, and an even better twist of taking pot shots at his own daughter to keep the secrets."

"So," Amy said, "Howell's attempt on Greta..."

"Points the way, my sweet friend and distinguished journalist-detective. It's got to be Greta. She got the disks from Dennis, and was the go-between to Howell."

"Why isn't Howell first on your list?"

"I wish he were, Amy. I truly wish he were. For his ideal of a pure white race, he would kill his own daughter. " I asked Amy to make sure Wales' office got copies of her notes, then I called Wales and laid it out for him.

"Peachart will need more proof for me to arrest her," Wales said.

I asked him to meet me at Stenopolis' home by noon. "And bring Peachart... if you have to cuff him and drag his ass out the door. I'll bring the video tape. I know we can prove this, Toby."

"We'll be there," he said.

I asked Amy to call Bob Able. "Just a courtesy. He's entitled to the endgame."

"See you there at noon," she said.

I drove out to the cabin, loaded the tape and let Jessie hop into the back of the truck and I stomped on the accelerator. But I had to stand on the brakes at the intersection of the bridge into Kootenai Falls and Second Street as a Dodge pickup sat blocking my entrance into the town. Out of the Dodge came Vreeland Peachart.

"Well," says Peachart, "how's my friend the former reporter? Enjoying your life of leisure?" He looked dapper for a change, wearing a beige corduroy jacket over a navy T-shirt, jeans and running shoes. He looked more like an NYU professor than a Montana county prosecutor. But — it was still Vreeland Peachart and no one should compare him to someone with brains and ethics.

"You're blocking me, Counselor."

"That I am. Well, seems like I'd like to have a little conversation, and you're a hard person to nail down." He sauntered over to me, then rested against my truck.

"Oh, I don't know, Vreeland. I seem to be the easiest target around. I get nailed, as you say, in the park in Taos, and asked to BACK OFF on the Internet. Was that you?"

"Doesn't slow you down much, though." He straightened up then. A few cars came by, slowly, edging as they could around us. "Say, why don't we go over to the VFW and have a drink?" he said. "We can talk over a few things, maybe smooth it out a little between us."

I waited a beat as though I was giving his invitation real consideration, then I said, "Let's talk right here. I'm in a hurry."

"That's what Detective Wales just told me over my radio. Says you have intentions of popping open our recent murder cases."

"You want to be governor of Montana, Peachart? Fine. But doing it over lies and cover-ups and sleazy dealings makes you such an ordinary kind of asshole politician."

"Hey, I understand," he said, smiling. "You're above it all. The big writer from New York, the moralist." He narrowed his eyes. "Big deal Peabody Award winner," he said, both hands out in front of him as though he were trying to stop a train.

"Everybody loves him," he said. "Everybody thinks he's on the side of good... the cat's ass, so to speak. But you have that little slut tucked back in your bedroom when you want her. And you seem not to be able to hold down a job for very long."

"You're talking about Ms. Kroll?"

"And maybe that little trollop you like so well in the Kootenai Falls Cafe´... little what's-her-name."

"Rita."

"And what else? There must be someone else. Out at the Red Dog, that bunch of...."

Jessie had been at the open back windows of the truck checking out whether or not her services might be needed. You could tell by the ears that she was in the plotting stages. I waved her off. No, I said to her, "It's okay, Jess."

Peachart looked the way I was looking, saw Jessie at the window and his face went white. "She touches me and you're in big trouble."

"No, Peachart, *you'll* be in big trouble."

"I don't want to hurt your dog."

"Don't worry, you won't. She won't give you the chance." I scowled at Jess and she grinned, and I said with firmness, "That'll do, Jessie." She understood, settled down on her bed, her ears cocked. I truly hoped she wouldn't take it upon herself to remove our county prosecutor's larynx. To Peachart I said, "So, do you want to listen to what I have?"

"My problem with you is something we'll have to settle another time," he said. "Right now, what we have in town here is a delicate situation. You and the rest of your kind in the media have no concern for the overall good of this community. You think all it takes is getting the headlines and to hell with the ramifications."

"That's what you people in..."

"Let me finish," he said, his index finger pointing at my forehead. "Oh, we need you press people. I don't fault you. But what is problematic here is that Hiram Howell may have been a despicable criminal in Germany, but the higher purpose for protecting a war criminal, if you will, is that our government decided officially that a greater good came about by getting critical information than by hanging him."

"It isn't up to you to decide who to protect."

He turned and walked to his truck then.

"You've got a point, Peachart," I said. "It's just not *my* point. There are a lot of people in this country who would not protect a man who marched people into death chambers, and who would probably do it again. You know about Howell's connection to the racists, I'm sure."

"You're an asshole, Moore!"

"And you're not governor material, Peachart."

# Chapter Thirty-One

Toby and I met out front where the silver sunlight came at us in spears. He had already spoken with Amy and was duly mystified that our government would stoop so low as to protect a man like Howell.

"I think there is no justification for that," I told him. "And I don't think any agency other than the CIA would do it."

He agreed. "Those FBI guys we brought in — they didn't check out."

"I thought they wouldn't."

"Looks like they broke a few laws on this one. Be hard to prosecute from here, though."

"Probably impossible," I said.

Toby looked up at the bright morning and sighed deeply.

Peachart showed up. I knew he would. There was no getting out of this now for him. As Amy and Bob Able parked, Toby and I went in and asked Alesandra to get Greta to come down into the living room. I carried the surveillance tape in front of me like a Christmas present.

This was the part I liked the least. Confrontation. Greta and Stenopolis had become friends over the weeks they'd been together. But this had to come. A recalcitrant prosecutor had to be shown that he had no way out but to re-open the case and charge Greta with first degree murder.

Greta came in with Stenopolis, and I began.

"We know about your father," I told her. "I have all the information about your relocations. I know you were born in 1953, and where. I know about the death of your brother at just a few hours after he was born.

She didn't flinch. Her eyes stayed with me, cold, resigned to what was coming.

"It's out now, Greta. We know about Gerhardt Gurster and what he did to Jews during the war in Germany."

Amy and Able walked in together. They had obviously heard. Peachart stood alone at the doorway, his face lined in worry.

"So this... *monster*... tries to kill his own daughter because she knows about the disks?" said Stenopolis. "And what was he in Germany?"

"He was in the camps. The Simon Wiesenthal people want him for war crimes against the Jews."

To Greta, I said, "Your father thought you were the last one who knew about the real software. With you dead, there would be no more people to talk."

Alesandra had her arm around Greta.

Toby looked at me.

Greta was not looking at me.

"There are a few things to clear up," I said. I asked Stenopolis if, after Leo told her about the surveillance equipment, she had said anything to Greta about it.

She looked at me without speaking, then said to Greta, "No. I don't believe it."

"So before Gil and Beth were killed, Leo, Dennis and you, Greta, were the only ones who knew about this," I said, pushing the video tape into the VCR across from Stenopolis' chair. "Until I told Bob Able here in this room about the surveillance equipment, even he didn't know about it."

There is something threatening about an object — any object — that is involved in a violent act, I think. I was counting on that — that something, some real object from the murder scene would have a palpable effect.

Greta nodded as though answering a question. It was truly an involuntary act.

"And when Amy and I viewed the tape, what did we see, Greta?"

"What's your point, Moore?" Peachart said.

Greta stared into my eyes and said nothing.

"We saw someone shooting Beth, bending over her after, and then standing and shooting Gil. And that someone was dressed in a disguise."

"So?" Peachart said, "you have a tape of a murder and a murderer who you cannot identify from the tape. Is that the evidence you are pushing here?"

I turned to Greta. "You learned about the new high-tech taping system from Dennis, didn't you, Greta?" She said nothing, so I went on. "Let's just play a little here. Let's see what we have."

Again, the stills of Beth seeming to run back toward the camera, away from the killer who is covered from head to foot.

Peachart said: "I've seen enough here. There is no reason to think the killer is anyone other than Dennis O'Brien. You said yourself he knew about the system."

Amy said: "Clearly if he were the murderer he would have

simply turned off the camera rather than risk being recognized, even in a disguise."

I turned to Greta. "The camera is so small. It fits into the palm of a hand like a cigarette lighter. It was in a clock above the entrance to the back room. So — if someone knew it was there but didn't know exactly where, it would be a problem.

"Leo, you knew it was there, but you didn't know where. Right?"

He nodded.

"And we can all see that the killer is taller than Leo. The killer is also..."

"Be kind, dear boy," Stenopolis said. "Yes, that image is of a much, um, thinner person than I, sad to say."

"That's you on this tape, Greta. And it was you who planted all that phony evidence against Dennis. You had to wear a disguise because you knew a tape would be made of you there and you couldn't spend the time looking for the camera. Dennis wouldn't have worn one, he would have turned the unit off.

"So I think we're out of people who knew about the surveillance system... with the exception of Hiram Howell... *after* the murders."

Stenopolis said, slowly, discovering her words on the way: "Which... is... why... YES. That's why he wanted to make an offer on the Red Dog. That would give him the time he needed to look for the camera and tape."

"That's if he wanted to protect Greta. And at that point, he did. Not until the CIA came back here and told him Dennis wasn't dead did he worry about Greta being discovered.

"Next item is the eagle feathers," I said, "supposedly a Hopi ritual. Well, everyone here thought Dennis was Hopi, including you, Greta. But I found out differently in Taos. But let's just keep that in mind for a minute.

"Now, the attempt on Greta by Howell. The key here is the so-called murder at the Laughing Horse Inn in Taos. The scene is set up, a local nut case is arrested for murder, and Dennis is spirited off by the CIA, or whatever agency. In exchange for his safe relocation, Dennis gives up the name of the security software buyer — Hiram Howell. Dennis has no idea Howell is in the Witness Protection Program. But the CIA or the marshals already knew Howell was active in the white supremacist movement. Howell probably was the biggest pain in the ass those agencies ever had. Now they know for certain he's going to be unveiled if the homicide investigation in Kootenai Falls continues. And now they want to make sure Howell isn't placed at center stage in the prosecutor's spotlight."

You could tell then that Greta had all but given up. She was limp, sat down and almost fell back in the chair and seemed not to be listening.

"Up here in Kootenai Falls, Howell, aka Gerhardt Gurster, sees his precious plan of secrecy coming apart. It's too risky for Hiram to do anything himself, like kill the only other person who knows what the real software can do. But this murderer of Jews, this racist, is a man of ideals. And maybe more important — there is a lot of money involved. A lot. But it is the ideal of the purity of a white race overcoming this mongrel country that drives him. If he can just erase Greta Hahn, aka Greta Howell...."

Peachart said: "You can prove that?

"I wouldn't be saying it if I couldn't, Counselor." As I spoke I reached down and froze the image of a large hat and trench coat firing a pistol toward the camera. "But what is important to understand is that Howell had to kill the only person, as far as he knew, who knew what the software really is, whether that be daughter, wife, mother... That part wasn't important. Even the CIA didn't know anything specific about the disks for a while, except that Howell was buying computer software and supplying to the National White Party."

Amy said to Peachart: "Howell had to kill Gil and Beth's killer to keep his secret. Lynette's execution was *by* Greta *for* Greta's protection. Am I right?" she said turning to me.

I nodded. Amy smiled. "How are we doing so far, Greta?" I said.

She seemed almost soft... until you thought back on the scene that Saturday at the Red Dog.

"Tell me if I go wrong here," I said to her. "Greta found out from Dennis what the deal was with the program and was told by the buyer — her father — that it would be a great opportunity to move his life's cause forward. He probably never mentioned murder, but how else could a completely secure system be secure? He left that to an adoring daughter to figure out for herself.

Toby said: "Clearly, unless the software developers were in Hiram's inner circle, the day they agreed to write the program was the same day they signed their own death warrants."

"Right," I said. I noticed that Peachart was not pleased at Wales siding with Amy and my analysis.

I said: "Setting up Dennis was easy. Either he'd be found guilty of murder — and who listens to a murderer? — or he'd run. If he ran, it would be simple, with Howell's connections, to eventually find him and kill him. I'm not sure how the plan went there, except that the set-up pretty much insured that Dennis would be locked up and, eventually executed.

"The problem, as we now know, was that neither Greta, nor anyone else here, knew that Dennis isn't Hopi."

Greta's eyes widened in surprise, and I went on. "He's from the Taos Pueblo. They're seen by some as direct descendants from the Anasazi Indians... meaning the ancient ones. Anasazis don't use eagle feathers or peyote. That is definitely Navajo or Hopi, but certainly not Anasazi. The killer made that very serious mistake there. That puts a spotlight directly on *set-up*.

"And the pretend rape? Obviously that was to throw off the investigation, point to a male. It was as crudely set up as the peyote and eagle feathers fiasco. The continuing problem here for Greta is that she has no facility for these things. Bottom line, Greta: you just aren't an accomplished murderer. I suspect too that there is a ton of forensic evidence that either was or could have been collected at the murder scene.

"The execution of Lynette was another part of the plan to misdirect. Greta was off supposedly at the Swan or Seeley Lake, over a hundred miles away. Our private investigator has verified that you were there," I said. Her eyes would not lock on to mine. "But it's only about a two-hour fast drive at best. And people on vacation often use their lodgings for day trips. So that alibi won't hold up. But that was brilliant — killing Lynette had the initial effect, anyway, of identifying Greta as a potential murder victim. From there it was simple to just plant the feathers at her own house, bury the gun at Dennis' place and then head back to the Swan. Oh, it's possible Hiram helped out here and there. He may have buried the revolver, in fact. But that's not the point."

I looked at Greta and said, pointing at the image on the TV screen, "You killed Gil and Beth and Lynette for your father... for the father you could not resist. He guaranteed you an easy life if this worked, and you loved him. You did it because of him. He is a strong man, isn't he, Greta? A strong, maybe even fierce man."

Peachart said, in a gesture of giving up his position, that she didn't have to say anything. Toby said: "I have to tell you that whatever you say...."

She managed to sit upright in a few moments, and when she spoke, her voice was low and steady.

"You are very wrong about him. He doesn't want to kill the whole world. He just wants people to live free with their own kind. He doesn't hate blacks or Jews or Indians or anybody." She stopped a moment and breathed deeply. "They should all be happier together with their own. It also could not have happened unless those Owens people were not so greedy. You haven't said anything about them. They were willing to help my father's cause... for money. They had no concern for what the cause was, they just wanted to be rich. They had no ethics and no morals. They just wanted money."

"And so — you killed for a father for nothing more than an idea."

She spoke through her crying: "You don't understand. It meant so much. His whole life. He was feeling his whole life fall in on him. I know he would never harm me if he were in his right mind." She sobbed for a moment, collected herself and said, "I forgive him. I love my father more than anything, and I forgive him."

"You forgive him, but you couldn't see him or talk to him like a father for... how many years? Protecting him was a whole life's commitment. How did he convince you to do that, Greta? How...."

"He was my father," she hissed. "He loved me. I couldn't live with him, but he was... so kind to me always."

Stenopolis moved toward Greta and I thought she was going to comfort her, put her arms around her. What she did was stand in front of Greta for a moment, and then raised her arm as if to slap her. "You're worse than the Nazis." She said nothing more, lowered her arm then, turned, looked at me, then slowly walked out of the room.

"And one more thing, Greta. You knew about the new security camera. Dennis told you about it, didn't he? That's why you had to disguise yourself as a man... because you didn't know where the camera was."

Greta nodded then and said she'd get her coat and go along with Toby, and Toby and I talked in the kitchen for a few moments while we waited.

"You realize that this is still pretty thin evidence...."

Peachart, standing behind us, said nothing. He was looking out of the back window, his eyes narrowed in thought.

"I understand," I said to Toby. "But you can see she's not going to fight it. This just lets you open the case and get the forensic report, and all of that. Besides, I think she's ready to sign a confession."

"Yes," he said, "but I doubt this tape would hold up in court or that Vreeland here will even prosecute, unless he gets a confession."

"You can bet on it," Peachart said.

"As for what we just heard, even Bob Able could get that

confession thrown out. What we need is solid forensic evidence. But," Toby said, thinking, "I'm going to take a chance and take her in. I'll drop the murder charges on Howell, even though we might be able to prove he planted evidence. But the assault charge sticks. I have witnesses."

"Oh?"

"If I can get them. Those phony FBI guys out there saw everything."

"Lots of luck, Toby. Those guys don't exist."

Toby and Peachart left then with Greta, and Stenopolis came down into the kitchen, her eyes sad. "She must be crazy, Brew. She doesn't yet understand that she killed real breathing human beings," she said. "As if Gil and Beth never existed. Some kind of game. You know?" she said. "We don't have any poisonous snakes in this part of Montana. We don't need them, we have each other."

"No, she knows what she did. That's both the sad and the terrible aspect of this. It's as if there is a legacy of Nazi DNA. It was a job that needed to be done."

"You understand it then?" Stenopolis said, looking off. "That must be a comfort."

"I understand how weak someone can be, but I'm always amazed what weakness can cause."

I went to my truck and my dog.

# Chapter Thirty-Two

Three days later, Greta Hahn — identified as Greta Howell — was arraigned for the murders of Gilbert and ElizaBeth Owen and Lynette Okla on the basis of forensic evidence — hair and threads from their clothing — along with the circumstantial evidence, mainly the surveillance tape, and also her knowledge of the software program. She was absolute stone, standing unmoved before the judge. She took a deep breath and, with Bob Able at her side, pleaded guilty.

Some weeks later, District Judge Dorothy Kolb sentenced her to eighty years for each homicide, to run concurrently. She could hope for possible parole by her seventy-fifth birthday.

After they took her away, Peachart paraded around as though he had had something to do with the real closing of the case.

As Greta left the courtroom, our eyes met. "Thank you," she said. I assumed that was something about finally being free of her father. But I'll always wonder.

In exchange for a suspended sentence, Hiram Howell, who never acknowledged that he was her father, agreed to be a witness for the prosecution. I found that easy to believe. It fit nicely with how he'd lived his whole life. But, he said, he'd do it only if necessary.

Peachart dropped charges against him.

There is no God.

I was present when Amy interviewed Howell for her story. He moved his hands through his silky white hair as he explained that, while he wanted a programmer to make a guaranteed secure communications system, he had no intention of breaking any laws, let alone seeing anyone get hurt. He added that if this country worked as it was supposed to, such extraordinary means to insure one's privacy would never be necessary.

"You know something," he said, "all of you think only the bad things about we Germans. But whatever the rules were, we followed them — to the letter. There would have been no possible way for some computer person — if they had had computers in those days — to help someone break our rules. A computer person who would work against his own government would be found out and punished. You Americans have rules, but you don't have the courage to make them stick."

He was forthcoming in his answers about his activities during World War Two. "I was a soldier and I did what soldiers do. If Germany would have won the war, your Dwight Eisenhower would have been tried for war crimes."

I turned away and tuned him out. I knew what was coming. We'd all heard it before, and I wasn't going to let him tell it to me again.

# Chapter Thirty-Three

Howell moved from Kootenai Falls, this time under his own power. The money he'd gotten from the disks must have been substantial. I guessed he might have gone somewhere south out of the country, as we heard that the Simon Wiesenthal Center had gotten a line on him. I keep looking for his name to show up on the wire, but so far it hasn't.

I phoned the FBI in Utah and told them I had copies of the original program disks, hoping they would be of use in their ongoing prosecution of subversion.

No one in the office seemed to know or care about them, so I gave them to Toby who said they'd be locked up forever with the evidence in the Hahn case.

In the end, things in Kootenai Falls sank back to small-town normal. Amy brought me back to the paper and Tom said that I had a job there again if I wanted it. I had to listen to ten minutes of just what kind of newspaper he was trying to run before I said I would come back and work in the office now and then on stories I chose to do — if he agreed to not pay me. For a while, I told him. I wasn't sure how long I wanted to stay on in my cabin that, unfortunately, I loved very much. But something had gone out of me; something had left and it all went flat at times, and uninteresting. And I didn't want to go on feeling like that.

I eventually wrote a story about prejudice and attitudes toward American Indians. It didn't attack Kootenai Falls or anyone, except it attacked us all. I was surprised when Tom let it go in. We received a few letters in response, but mostly the piece went unread.

Amy's story didn't make it past Tom's desk and was cut to shreds by the rewrite desk at the Associated Press. Kate apologized but said the world isn't interested in murderers who plead guilty. The only interesting thing about the story — Howell being Greta's father — had to be cut because it didn't make it to the court so it was not an official, reportable fact, according to the AP lawyers. Though it could be proved, they didn't want to take any chances with getting into litigation.

Also, Howell's origins and war crimes and his connection with the Witness Protection Program didn't make the story. I asked Kate if the CIA had anything to do with that. "I would hate to think so," she said. She said she was less paranoid than I am; that one of those rushed editors just didn't see why the AP had to "open up that can of worms."

"We'd have another good story if we could prove that the CIA or FBI pressured your editor, wouldn't we?" I said.

I heard from Wales that Allard in Taos had been let go. "They wanted it both ways," Toby said. "No corpse and a suspect in custody. But we put a little pressure on them."

The Letwiligs continue as the Letwiligs. Except that after all of his training, Kellog planned to enlist some friends and go down to Tijuana to find his brother, Shorty. That may be a healthy use for his camo training.

Big Jim moved in with a neighbor lady for a while, until she started talking about marriage.

Rita down at the Kootenai Falls Cafe´ quit and went to work at the health center. She grew more beautiful every day. But I was reminded of the poet Dee Snodgrass' line: Each year the young girls bloom farther and farther out of reach.

I said good-bye to Amy a month later. She had been looking around for a better reporting job and had decided to take an offer from a good daily over on the Oregon coast as a feature writer on its Sunday edition. I told her that it was okay with me. It was the kind of lie that she would try to believe and so would I. But it was time. I was getting along too well with her, and she with me, I suppose. But it felt in my gut as though I hadn't eaten in a week.

"I'll come over and see you," I told her.

"And I'll be back. It's not all that long a drive."

Then there was the moment when she looked down at the steering wheel as she turned it, backing away. She stopped, rolled down the window and leaned out. "I love you," she said.

I watched her drive off, slipping my hands into my pockets to stop their shaking. I watched the back of her old Volvo grow smaller as it moved down the road. I thought, how strange that it grows smaller and the heaviness in me grows larger. I watched until there was nothing left to see and then it seemed to me that it wasn't enough of a good-bye. I turned back to the house and saw Jessie sitting at the front door, looking at the road.


No one in Kootenai Falls ever again heard from Dennis O'Brien. But I spoke with Len in Taos on the phone one afternoon who said he saw someone who looked like Dennis out at the Pueblo, and when he asked his friend who it was, the reply was, "That's a man called Red Feather. I've never spoken to him and he has never spoken to me." Len said Red Feather had recently returned and was living the way his ancestors had... drawing water from the stream mornings, living without electricity. "If it's Dennis, he's okay," Len said.

Vreeland Peachart abandoned his dream of running for governor and left Kootenai Falls to join a cousin in Colorado as a partner in a telemarketing business.

Bob Able was appointed Acting County Attorney.

I never mentioned Able's style of representing Dennis O'Brien to him or anyone ever again. He made a pretty good public prosecutor, admirably smothering his racist nature, and as long as I didn't have to spend time with him, it was all right with me that he decided on public life.

Jessie won third place in a sheepdog trial in Bozeman in early July. By mid-summer, after working our sheep twice a day, in between my own serious late night bouts at the Red Dog, she had taught me enough so that I planned to enter her in a major trial in California in September.

After her victory, Jessie and I took a trip up the road into British Columbia to Lake Kootenay at Ainsworth Hot Springs and slept lakeside, she on her round bed, and I slept more soundly than I had in months tucked into my L.L.Bean sleeping bag under a frightening number of stars. I woke once to the shrill singing of coyotes, but that was all right. It was clear air and quiet after that, and we pretended it was wild and without people. When I woke in the morning, I saw her looking down at me. She had been watching me sleep.

We stayed there a while listening to the lake and the birds as the light grew. The mountains across the lake were gray camels draped in a golden haze, and I told her of our plans to work sheep in California. We were quiet then, sitting together dreaming of other mountains.

After a while she lay her head down against my arm and listened to me talk, her ears flat back against her head, her head moving occasionally. I touched the side of her warm face with my hand and she pressed against it for a long moment, but then she stood, stretched her neck and chin out, and looked sharply at me, her ears cocked in expectation. It was time to get the hell up, she was saying, and it was indeed time, she was saying, to get the hell on the road and look for an adventure.

Later that same week, during a walk with Jessie at Yaak

County Park, some ten miles up the road from our cabin, an invisible thermal swept over a grassy, weedy area the size of a football field. I heard nothing and felt nothing. It was a silent twister coiling upward but leaving the rest of the area undisturbed, the kind of wind you see in deserts that we call dust devils. But here there was no dust. Instead, dozens of straw-colored, Frisbee-size, long-stemmed seed pods broke loose and rose up, circling as hawks and eagles do. Long-stemmed pods, looking like so many rising umbrellas, circling higher and higher, one above the other, until one moved too far to the outer rim of the rising funnel. It tipped over and fell slowly to the side as the others rose up and out of sight.

Well, I thought — you just never know.

I stood for a while, Jessie out in front, waiting, and wondered what it felt like to be snatched up and flown away without warning.

That night I went to the Red Dog. There was no one around except Teri and Ellen, so we had Jessie in for a minute. She turned around a few times and then settled at the feet of my bar stool. Ellen put a mug of Moose Drool in front of me. The radio was crackling some ungodly, repetitious, thumping song with lyrics that sounded like an avalanche.

"What if I wanted something else for a change?" I said, talking over the radio. "Like maybe a Coors instead of this," pointing to the mug, "and maybe some jazz on that damned radio."

Ellen stood in front of me, one hand on her hip, shook her head in her best Mae West impression, and said, "Drink your Drool, boy."

I took a sip as instructed and checked Jessie who was pretending sleep. I would stay awhile with friends, go home and call Kate, and tomorrow it would be a step closer to new snow on the peaks around us all.

In bed later, I thought of that last night with Amy. It had been a rainy evening. It had rained all night and was raining lightly in the morning. I woke early and lay next to her listening to the rain. Later, when there was a dim light growing from the east-facing window, she moved, touched my leg, then turned onto her back and the sound the covers made was the same as the rain. I did not think about her driving off and I did not think about her kissing me one final time. I did not think these things, only of the rain and the light growing now across her hair, and her arms over me and my mouth on her cheek, no thoughts of anything except the rain and the light and her hair against me. I thought of nothing. She kissed me once as if rising from a dream, and then we rolled apart and slept.

JOHN HERRMANN was born in Berkeley, California. He received the MFA degree in writing from the University of Iowa Writers' Workshop and later became the first director of the MFA program at the University of Montana, Missoula. He taught for over twenty years at many universities and colleges in the U.S. and abroad, and his stories have appeared in *North American Review, Northwest Review, South Dakota Review, Western Review, Twilight Zone, Murderous Intent Mystery Magazine*, and many others, several earning honors in *Best American Short Stories, Best American Mystery Stories* and *Best Little Magazine Fiction*. His biography appears in the current *Who's Who in America*.

Currently, he lives with his border collie, Mackie, in a small log house in a remote area of northwest Montana.

## The Cover Artist

RAVEN O'KEEFE is a Montana artist who specializes in portraits of border collies. Her friends John Herrmann and Mackie have inspired many pieces of her art, and will surely inspire more, as they inspire joy in her life.